all the wrong PAGES

KATHERINE MCINTYRE

Cover design by: Ethereal Designs

Editing: Rebecca Fairfax

Printed in the United States of America

Contents

To Brian—thanks for Portland!

Acknowledgements

This shared world was such a blast to splash around in! I'm so glad I got to work with the other authors in the creation of this small town, and I thoroughly enjoyed being a part of this series. All the brainstorming and figuring out the details of what made up Collier's Creek was so fun with this crew! To Elle, Becca, Nic, Sue, and Ali—I adore your creativity!

For All the Wrong Pages, I owe a huge thanks to Melissa, Julie, Elle, Nic, and Becca for beta reading this book to make sure it was a fun installment in the Collier's Creek series. Always a shout out to my author friends and my reader group for putting up with my whining about keeping secrets. A huge thanks as well to Rhys at Ethereal Designs for the amazing job with the cover and to Rebecca for her sharp editorial skills.

And as always, a thank you to my wonderful friends and family for all the support and encouragement—I wouldn't be able to do any of this without you.

Chapter One

Cooper

I was going to kill Logan Nichols.

Irritation percolated through my veins as I tore down the "Honk if you love dick" banner he'd plastered across the front of my tiny shop. Ellis Leatherworking worked as the central hub to peddle my trade while also sourcing the handyman jobs that had always been my bread and butter. It was also an easy target when you had a pest like Logan who had been pranking you ever since high school—a full decade ago.

A honk sounded as a blue pickup truck I recognized drove by, and I lifted a middle finger. Nash was probably heading into town to grab something for the ranch at this hour.

I peeled at the tape at the edge of the banner, yanking the rest of it from the front of the building. The worst of all was I could already picture Logan's twinkling eyes the next time I ran into him, the insatiable smirk because yet again he'd found a way to piss me off.

My temper wasn't that terrible—okay, I wouldn't win awards for patience—but somehow Logan stripped my wires more than any other human on the planet. It was like someone had designed the antithesis of my personality and plunked them right in the middle of our tiny-ass town. I carried the banner over to the trash and unceremoniously tossed it in before heading into my shop. Unlike obnoxious dicks who didn't have anything better to do than annoy me, I had work to get done.

Not only did I have a few orders of specialty leather bracers to fulfill from a few tourists who had come into town, but I had a full day of fixing lightbulbs and hooking up dishwashers for the elderly citizens of Collier's Creek. The Ellis family had been here when the town was founded, and we ran the town bookstore, on top of being known for the leatherworking trade in town for years. My dad might've left the craftsman life behind with his accounting business, but I was determined to keep the leatherworking shop alive.

Only problem was, apart from the occasional birthday and Christmas presents and the tourists that came through, it had been a tough industry to stay afloat in as of late.

A knock pounded at my door, and I groaned. It was too early to deal with anyone, especially after walking up to find the exterior of my shop vandalized, yet again, by Logan. And Sheriff Morgan didn't seem to care in the slightest.

Maybe because the guy was too focused on Geraldine's 911 calls about the neighbor's dog getting possessed for the thousandth time. Barkasaurus Rex wasn't possessed, just hyper as shit, but she kept swearing he barked in tongues.

Or maybe the sheriff didn't give a damn since this feud between Logan and I had been going on for so long that no one in the town cared anymore.

Except me.

The knock pounded again, just as loud.

I hauled myself up and headed to the door. The quick turn of the knob revealed the familiar face of my best friend.

"Oh, you." I wrinkled my nose and tried to shut the door again.

"Thought you'd need coffee this morning," Kai said, the gleam in his eye giving him away. The man was Greek-model gorgeous, even at this hour, with tousled brown hair and smooth olive skin. I'd propositioned him in the past, but unfortunately for me, he was as straight as they came. He lifted two cups of coffee from CCs, which was a godsend but suspicious as fuck.

"How'd you know about the sign?" I asked, crossing my arms and not wasting time with wondering as I sank into a lean against the doorframe.

"Worked a late shift last night," Kai said, a shit-eating grin spreading across his face. "Saw Logan tacking it up, and so I stopped to chat for a few minutes."

I sucked in a deep breath, not budging from my spot at the doorframe. "No heads-up? No warning? What sort of best friend are you?"

Kai muscled his way in past me, his jabby elbows enough to get me to move as he navigated with the coffee. "The kind who knows how much you value your sleep and figured this would be more welcome in the aftermath."

Well, hell. He wasn't wrong.

"You still could've shot a text or something," I muttered, following the alluring scent of coffee that wafted from the to-go cups.

"And miss your grumpy-as-fuck reaction?" Kai said, popping the cups of coffee on my desk, half-covered in paperwork for orders and invoices from vendors. He plunked down into my beaten leather chair I needed to reupholster. Not like shabby furniture made my business look great. "You know," Kai continued, "if you didn't flip out every time Logan pulled one of his pranks, he'd stop doing them. Coop, half the town thinks you're secretly in love with the guy."

I shot him a glare. "That's a fuck no. What am I supposed to do? Let him vandalize my business, my home, and ruin my dates without saying something?"

Kai rolled his eyes. He was lucky he'd brought me coffee.

"Look, finding someone to date around here is hard enough without Logan either swooping in and stealing prospective hookups for the night or interrupting my dates over at Jake's Tap. Not all of us can marry our high school sweethearts, Kai."

He shrugged and took a sip from his coffee like it wasn't a big deal, but the man had the rock-solid relationship with Shelby that I envied. "I know you'll find someone. You've always been a catch."

"Who can't seem to keep a relationship alive," I muttered, leaning against the desk and drinking a gulp from my cup. Heat seared my mouth—wrong move. Girlfriends and boyfriends alike got tired of me—said I was too stuck in my ways, too stubborn. They weren't wrong, but I didn't know how to be any different. And the years ticked by while I continued to strike out, the worry turning into a steady buzz under my skin.

Almost as steady as the worry over my shop.

"Psh, when you find the right one..." Kai started and didn't finish. He knew I'd heard the line from every single member of my family a thousand times. The Ellises were not only a close bunch but also nosy as hell, and I got a regular running commentary every time I showed up to an event without a date. Which was often.

"When I find the right one, they'll dump me too. Or move to Portland." I glanced at the invoice on the table and tried to ignore the glaring numbers of what was owed—far more than I brought in at the moment.

"Cassie last year was what, number three?" Kai said, his eyes twinkling in amusement as he continued to sip at his coffee.

"I'm glad my misery entertains you. Something about me clearly says stepping stone to a life in Portland."

Two girlfriends and a boyfriend had broken up with me to go find themselves in Portland, Oregon, to the point I was starting to believe I was cursed. Or they'd all discussed amongst each other and agreed on this breakup tactic. Our town was one grocery store and two gas stations kind of small, so word spread fast.

"Should be part of the contract they sign upon dating you," Kai said. "Have no secret longing to go to Portland."

"Yeah, well no one's going to be showing any interest when Logan's tacking up "Honk if you love dick" signs to my business. Like we needed to scare away more potential customers." My jaw clenched on automatic, and I resisted the urge to grip my flimsy paper coffee cup too hard. Instead, I took another swig, this one marginally cooler and less mouth-burning.

"Speaking of interest," Kai said, "I was doing one of my feed deliveries to a ranch in the neighboring town, and their normal leatherworker is out on injury at the moment. They're going to be hitting you up for repair work soon."

I hated the relief that rolled through me there. Despite my determination to keep the family business going—one that had been a historical part of this town for well over a hundred years—I was running into pitfalls.

The largest problem being the supply source, which was dwindling.

"Thanks for keeping an eye out," I said, my tone a little too gruff. Vulnerability of any sort I loathed, but the idea of the family business collapsing like so many others around Collier's Creek gutted me.

"How are things really going?" Kai asked, dropping his voice.

I didn't look up, mostly because I didn't want to catch his serious gaze fixed my way. My family saw the strong front, heard about any big new orders and whatever wins I had to celebrate. I couldn't stand the idea of letting them down, of losing all our history in one fell swoop.

I took a sip from the coffee before responding. "Steady decline for the last three years. At this point, my handyman jobs are the sole profit keeping me afloat here. If I don't find a source of leatherworking income soon, this will just be a glorified hobby."

There were worse things, I was well aware, but hell. Uncle Ray had taught me the ropes of the trade he'd spent his whole life perfecting, and I'd been doing this since high school. Leatherworking was something we had shared together before he passed—a fucking drunk driver, an out-of-towner, had hit him on his way back from work. The idea of letting the leatherworking business go felt like a slap in the face to everything he'd taught me.

"Shit, Coop," Kai swore. "Why the hell haven't you reached out to anyone? Does your family know?"

"No, and you're not going to say anything," I responded, dosing myself with more caffeine. Why the hell not. The day had already started out in the dumpster—as evidenced by the crumpled signs in my trash can—so why not add emotional flagellation to the mix before I finished my first coffee? Normally, I evaded these types of conversations, but with the sharper decline in business as of late, I either needed to get creative, or Ellis Leatherworking would be no more.

"The rest of your family would be pounding at your door to help in a second." Kai raised a brow at me.

"I'm not about to make my problems their problems," I shot back, crossing my arms over my chest. My skin prickled at the idea of asking for assistance. Out of the family, I'd always been the one to come up with solutions, not cause trouble, and I wouldn't start being a burden on them now.

Kai shook his head. "You know they wouldn't view it that way."

"Look, I just need to land some bigger orders, and I'll be fine," I said, lying like it earned me money. However, the more we continued this conversation, the more we faced how fucked I was, and I wasn't prepared to handle my future reality. "Even better, get Logan to stop disparaging my business."

"You need to get laid, man." Kai tipped back more of his coffee. "You're fucking brimming with tension."

"I'll make that the top of my agenda."

Better focusing on a hookup than the fact I was a few bad months away from closure.

Chapter Two

Logan

"One of these days, Coop's going to flat-out murder you," Penny said, helping herself to the seat across from me. As if she belonged there or something—though, she pretty much did.

I'd been coming to CCs on a regular basis since I started getting the occasional freelance editing job on top of my hours at the bookstore. Working at home—my aunt's house—was a less than peaceful experience ever since I bought a cockatiel on a whim, one that Aunt Beth threatened to let out in the wild. However, Jim Squawkins was a fixture in my life, and I refused to rehome him, even if his incessant noises sometimes made my ears bleed. I had never been a bird person before, but I was trying it out.

"He wouldn't resort to murder." I leaned back in my seat, nudging my laptop to the side so I could see my best friend better. "That wouldn't look good on his Perfect Citizen Resume. He'll just grumble a lot, shoot me some dirty looks."

Penny blew on the top of her tea, the furls of steam rising up. Her auburn hair drifted down her shoulders, barely held back by a clip. "You say that, but I don't want to be attending your funeral because you couldn't keep your pranks in your pants."

I snorted and took a sip of my cappuccino, rich and foamy and in a large enough mug to last me a while. The door to CCs swung open, Ben Johnson, the local dispatcher, walking in, probably to get his usual as well as something for the sheriff—his now boyfriend. CCs was a picturesque coffee shop, straight out of a fairytale. White walls, pine tables, and black chairs created a harmonious interplay, and light radiated through the place, encouraged by the wide, welcoming windows.

"Look, Coop might not like my pranks, but the rest of the town appreciates them," I said, placing a hand over my chest.

Cameron, the owner of CCs, stood behind the counter, casting his magic on the espresso machine as he made drinks for Ben. We were seated in the booth closest to the handoff pane, which meant he was in listening distance—most likely to his regret.

"You like my pranks, right, Cameron?" I called out.

Cameron glanced up, a smirk rising to his lips. "As long as they don't involve my shop, sure."

"Are you talking about the dick sign you put up this morning?" Ben asked as he sauntered over to the handoff pane. "Because he was fuming about that."

I rested my elbows on the table and my chin on my hands before fluttering my lashes. "Tell me more."

Penny reached across the table and thwacked me in the shoulder, like a monster. "No, don't tell him more. He doesn't need encouragement."

"Was he stomping around his shop? Cursing up a frenzy?" I asked, greedy for details. Nothing was hotter than Cooper Ellis when he got irritated and started ranting. Those insanely blue eyes would be flaring, his firm mouth would be in a scowl, and his crossed arms would make all those muscles bunch. The man was the sort of pulse-pounding gorgeous that had drawn my eyes since we were pre-teens and I first started noticing boys.

Yes, he was the longest crush I'd ever had—fifteen years and counting.

Yes, he also hated my guts, so I was well aware nothing would ever come from my hundreds of fantasies.

However, I refused to pass up free eye candy.

"Nash said he was pissed as hell while he was tearing down the signs," Ben responded, unable to hide the amusement in his eyes.

"What possessed you to hang a "Honk if you love dick" banner at his shop?" Penny asked. "Hasn't the poor man suffered enough?"

"Come on now," I said, tapping my finger against the wooden surface of the table. "You've been giving him a pass because you feel guilty over something that happened in high school."

Penny wrinkled her nose. "Maybe a little. But he's such a sweetheart. We already hurt him back then by dating after I broke up with him, so why keep antagonizing?"

Because I want to hop on his dick.

I licked my lips. As much as half the town had figured out the heart-shaped boner I had for Cooper Ellis, for some reason my sweet, naïve best friend hadn't. I didn't bother telling her because she'd only blame herself since our cover-up relationship had started the feud. "You know, this is why you keep missing when every hot girl tries to flirt with you."

"Here's your order, Ben," Cameron said, passing him the coffees. "Better rush off quick before Logan can drag you into more of his childish attempts at hitting on Coop."

Penny rolled her eyes, like she didn't believe Cameron. For fuck's sake, the girl had no radar. Her future wife would pretty much have to pussystamp her to get her interest across.

"You were the kid who kicked the boys you liked on the playground, weren't you," Cameron mused.

I sniffed. "I'm not going to justify that with an answer. Besides, what makes you think I'd be the playground bully, with a waifish frame like this?"

"It's true," Penny said. "He's always been pocket-sized."

"Five foot seven is not pocket-sized," I argued. "Just because you come from a family of giants." Penny and her family considered anything below five foot eight subpar, which was frankly offensive to normal people.

The door swung open again, this time Geraldine appearing with her mangy little fluffball, Barkasaurus Rex, in her arms. She claimed the dog was a purebred Bichon Frise, but whoever sold her the dog had lied. It looked like a cross between a Pomeranian and a French bulldog who chain-smoked on the regular.

"Excuse me," Cameron said with a grin. "I've got a business to run."

"Good luck with that," I muttered, glancing at my laptop screen. My email was pulled up, and I had a new one in my inbox. I skimmed the subject line.

Re: Remote Work Opportunity

My heart kicked into double time. I'd been applying for full-time jobs on the downlow, even though I didn't want to leave Ellis Bookshop. I loved working at the bookstore, but I needed more income. The bills that formed a constant yoke around my shoulders weren't disappearing any time soon, and Larry Ellis could only afford to pay so much. The idea of quitting the bookstore made me feel sick though. If I could find the perfect combination—maybe enough freelance editing jobs to still work shifts at the bookstore—but the freelance editing jobs were hard to come by, and a full-time salaried position might take some of the stress off my shoulders.

"What's making you so serious?" Penny asked, nudging my ankle with her foot under the table.

"I had looked into this CSA remote work job." I scrubbed my palms over my face before clicking open the email.

"You mean leaving the bookstore?" Penny asked, her voice too damn loud.

"Shh," I responded as I skimmed over the contents of the email.

Blah, blah, blah—*Would like to set up an interview*—Sincerely, Blah.

My pulse picked up pace, and I drummed my fingertips over the tabletop. Was I doing this? Applying for different jobs felt like a betrayal of Gramps and all the kindness he'd shown me. Not my grandfather, Cooper's actually, but he had insisted I call him Gramps. And considering the sole family I had left in the area was my aunt who I lived with but barely talked to, I leapt at the chance for those connections. Besides, Grandpa Ellis had the best taste in books—a genre junkie like me—and he kept his place lively with book clubs, local author visits, and cheese and wine nights in peak tourism seasons.

"You going to answer me or just keep me in suspense?" Penny asked before taking another sip of her tea.

"Look, I don't know," I said, hissing out a sigh. I should set up the interview. The money would be enough that maybe I'd be able to move out on my own. Aunt Beth was fine with me living with her, but we'd never been the sort of close I'd hoped for from my only remaining relative. Mom had raised me on her own, and when she died five years ago, I'd been picking up the pieces ever since. My stomach squeezed tight.

My whole life had upturned when Mom passed—and I wished it had just been the grief, but I'd co-signed on a card to pay for some of the immediate cancer treatments, and those remaining bills were...well, fuck. I was floundering.

Penny reached across the table to squeeze my hand. "Hey. Do what you need to. Mr. Ellis will understand either way."

I chewed back a scream. He might, but this would be yet another upheaval. I had so little to call my own, so little to cling to that losing any more would break me at the knees. My gaze snagged on the salary of the CSA position, which was a hell of a lot higher than anything paid around here due to the New York City location and pharma business.

"Thanks, Pen," I said instead of airing anything roiling around in my brain. Stupid pranks on Cooper Ellis were a hell of a lot simpler than this shit. I gritted my teeth and opened a reply email. In a few minutes, I had a response crafted, and I sent out the email asking to set up the interview.

Dreams could wait.

"Gina showed up in my book again," Penny said, redirecting the conversation, thank fuck. "Like, two weeks since her last appointment and for another haircut?"

Penny worked at Divine Style, one of the older salons in the area, and she'd been cutting hair ever since high school. Girl was fucking good at it—just trash at picking up when someone was hitting on her.

"Is she cute?" I asked, taking another sip of my cappuccino.

Penny nibbled on her lower lip. "Um, yes. Punky with a side shave and a lumberjack vibe going on."

'I bet you money if you asked her out she wouldn't say no," I said, giving her an arch look.

Penny let out a little huff. "Not every woman is hitting on me, Logan."

"Just most," I responded.

The door swung open, and Kyle, one of the guys who owned the hardware store across the street from Ellis Books strode in. "Logan?" He locked in on me, and my spine stiffened at the seriousness in his tone. That couldn't spell good news, and unfortunately, I was far too well-acquainted with the bad sort.

"What's going on?" I asked, hesitation sticking my words.

"Larry's in the hospital."

My stomach dropped. Grandpa Ellis was in trouble.

Chapter Three

Cooper

I got the call while I worked at Ms. Hendricks's, fixing her light-bulbs.

Grandpa had gotten rushed to the hospital. Mom had taken the time to explain it was just a broken leg, not anything life-threatening, but I still left the job with a quick explanation. Ms. Hendricks understood—she had been friends with my grandmother for years before she passed, and she maintained a solid friendship with my grandfather. My heart thumped hard, and I pumped the gas pedal as I soared down the highway. Thank fuck our backwater wasn't so remote that we had to drive far to Collier's Creek Hospital. It might be small, but it was in town.

Fifteen minutes later, I pulled in front of the hospital and skidded into a parking spot. I hopped out, my palms a little sweaty. Grandpa might be fine, but a broken leg still had hazards, especially at his age. And knowing him, he'd resist help and try to get around the rest the doctor would tell him to take.

Sue, the usual intake nurse behind the desk, waved me back. "He's on the second floor, room 205, and already trying to crawl out of here."

I rolled my eyes, trying to mask the shaky relief that cascaded through me at her casual comments. While Mom said Gramps was fine, it was one thing hearing the statement from her and another hearing from the medical team. Only a few people slouched around in the lobby, most of them unfamiliar faces, which meant out-of-town-ers. Grow up in a place like this with a family like mine and you were guaranteed to know every single person in town. It didn't hurt that both of my jobs put me front and forward with the community.

Some days, all the nosiness, gossip, and scheming from the townies drove me crazy. Other times, I loved living somewhere where support was an arm's reach away. Too bad I didn't reach for it.

I hiked up the short staircase, the weathered black rubber treads squeaking. Once I hit the second floor, it took all of two seconds to locate Gramps's room—the one with my two youngest siblings loitering about. Sadie and Henry's attention swung my way at once. Both of them had the same dark hair my father did, like I had, but Henry also received my father's features, hard and square. Sadie's came from my mother—fine boned, narrow nose, while I got a blend of the two, square jaw and narrow nose.

"How were we the ones to get here first?" Sadie said, arching a brow. Already, nearing the door, I could hear the sounds of Mom and Grandpa bickering, which told me he was fine. Silence was the deadliest thing in this family.

"I was on a job at the opposite side of town," I responded, slight irritation percolating through me that I hadn't gotten here before my other siblings. Did I take the oldest brother position a little too seriously sometimes? Well, yes, but someone needed to rein this unruly bunch in. Henry didn't need as much watching over as he used to, and Daisy had kids of her own to take care of, but Sadie and Jordan left a steady stream of howling puppies and chaos wherever they went.

"What are you waiting for then?" Henry gestured toward the door. "Break up whatever argument they're having."

I unclenched my jaw to heave a sigh before striding into Gramps's room.

Gramps had the sort of face that would scare a baby—a beak of a nose, hard blue eyes, the jawline he'd passed down to my dad. Except the moment the man spoke, when he broke into a smile, he emitted such warmth it drew everyone in. Nothing like me. Right now, however, he was more in the Scaring a Baby camp with his bushy brows knotted together.

"I can go home tonight," he argued, and I withheld my eye roll.

"Not based on what Doctor Crane said," Mom responded, her arms crossed in a brick-wall stance. Dad might be Gramps's son, but demeanor-wise, my mother acted more like him by far.

"You don't want us having to drive you back here in the middle of the night, do you?" I asked, jumping in at my own peril. But Gramps had a soft spot for his grandkids and wouldn't give us nearly the shit he would Mom and Dad.

"You wouldn't have to," he grumbled, lying back against the white pillows, his leg in a splint and elevated. "Because I'd be doing just fine at home."

I pointed to his leg. "While you're on crutches and hobbling around your two-story house? You'd save us more time by staying the recommended night and then letting one of us get you home."

Gramps set his jaw, the stubbornness an inherent trait in the Ellis family. His pride I knew well because it was my own.

"I already rushed over here the second I heard something happened," I said, laying on the guilt with a putty knife. "You go home early and we'll all just be repeating this."

Mom bit back her smile, and Gramps fixed me a no-nonsense look that said he saw right through my bullshit—but it gave him the out his pride needed.

"Fine," he muttered. "We can tell Doctor Crane I'll stay the night. But you lot better be prepared for some phone calls to save me from the boredom of this place. The only working station on this TV is the Home Shopping Network. I hate all forms of shopping."

"Apart from book shopping," Mom said, passing him a wry glance. "And Len's grabbing dinner right now, so we can all set up camp here."

"Are you sure that won't be a noise violation?" Henry asked as he strolled inside. "If Jordan ever arrives and Daisy shows up with her circus troupe, we're cramming close to fifteen in this tiny room."

"What, you think Dr. Crane is going to give a damn?" Gramps responded.

"No, but I figure Sue will get fed up with the back-and-forth shuffle as well as a laundry list of complaints from out of towners," Henry responded.

"Live a little, son," Mom said, saving us all the trouble. Henry used to be such a risk-taker as a kid, but the older he got, the more he clung to rules and order with every turn. "We've got history here, and Sue's not going to kick our family out for sharing a dinner with Gramps."

The phrase got uttered so often it might as well be stamped on my bones—"we've got history here" was so damn true. The Ellis name on businesses in Collier's Creek and the work we contributed was an asset to most of the townies here. And the piece of history I'd been clutching on to—the leatherworking trade in town—was a constant presence, a reminder of why I couldn't lose it.

A commotion sounded from down the hall, which meant Jordan had arrived. My younger brother always appeared in a whirlwind of cursing and cigarettes, and he probably would've checked his phone by now—though with him, it could sometimes take days.

A guy burst through the door to Gramps's room, but it wasn't my brother.

Irritation flushed through me on reflex.

Logan's blond hair was windswept, his dark brown eyes intense as he strode past me, clearly in a rush. He wore a pale blue polo that made his tan skin pop and skinny black jeans so tight they showcased everything—legs for miles and an ass so bouncy the fabric could barely contain it. If I checked out his peachy backside a bit too often, then it was simply tax for having to deal with him in the first place.

The man might be annoying as sin, but anyone with eyes could see he was gorgeous.

Of course he'd show up. We had this handled—after all, the family had showed up in full force, but ever since Gramps adopted him into the fold, Logan appeared everywhere. It was bad enough I couldn't avoid him around town, but I couldn't even avoid him at family gatherings now. He appeared with a cheeky grin and some snarky comments lobbed my way, ones the rest of my family found *hilarious*. He wasn't funny. He was a menace.

"Gramps, are you okay?" Logan asked, clear worry ringing in his voice, and guilt crept in. Even if he annoyed the hell out of me, his care for my grandfather was genuine. And considering the amount of time they spent together working at the bookshop, it made sense he'd be here.

I took a few steps back, not wanting my own feud with Logan to cloud Gramps's time with him. Particularly the sign on my building that needed addressing. Last thing I needed was to scare more customers away—I was already hard up for them.

Logan rushed right to Gramps's side, ignoring me for once. "I came as soon as I heard."

"Pfft," Gramps said. "Everyone's acting like it's a stroke when all I have is a damn broken leg."

"At your age—" Mom started, and he lifted a hand.

"Don't even finish your sentence, Mary."

Logan's shoulders descended from their tight hunch. "You were trying to pull a Belle from *Beauty and the Beast*, weren't you."

Gramps broke out into the widest grin, and for a moment, any of my irritation at Logan vanished. Sometimes, for a brief instant, my gut tugged with this longing for that effortless ability Logan had to brighten people's days—even though he only put a damper on mine.

"You caught me," Gramps said. "Look, you can't have a bookstore and not sail across the book stacks on a rolling ladder."

"Right, so you don't mind if I try?" Logan asked, his eyes twinkling with mischief.

"Once I'm healed up, sure," he said. "Can't have two of us out on a broken ankle."

Logan chewed his lower lip. "How should we handle that?"

"Oh, it'll just be a week," Gramps said, waving at him.

"That's not true in the slightest," I jumped in, my arms crossed. Logan better not start guilting my grandfather into coming in to work before he was ready.

"Are you operating on a different time system again?" Logan ignored me and kept up with his infuriatingly cheeky tone. "I have it on good authority that leg breaks take a bit longer than a week to heal."

"By good authority, do you mean the time you fractured your tibia after O'Connell's graduation party?" I muttered.

"God, you remember that?" he asked. "It's like you're obsessed with me."

"How could I forget," I responded, my hand clenching into a fist. "You somehow broke it tripping over my parked car. It took me weeks to get the dent out."

"I still say you pulled a bit of a hit-and-run there," he responded, his grin ever-present. *Nothing* on this planet got me heated like this man.

"Who fucking hit you?" I asked. "The car was parked. No one was in it. And you sure as hell weren't running with a broken tibia."

"Coop, we're in a hospital," Henry commented, tilting his head toward the door.

I clenched my jaw and resisted the urge to murder both my brother and Logan.

"I'm aware," I responded. "One that's going to be awash with noise anyway when the rest of the family gets here."

"Should I put out a notice for part-timers at the store?" Logan asked, switching gears back to Gramps at a lightning speed. He always did this, to the point where I got whiplash.

A frown wrinkled Gramps's features. "By the time we train them or find them, I'll be working again."

The idea of Gramps being back in the shop after a week or two would give me an ulcer. Mom's shoulders scrunched up, like she might burst into a doozy of a fight with Gramps. That was the last thing we needed right now.

"I'll help out," I said, before I realized words had escaped me. Ones I honestly regretted. But while the handyman jobs remained steady, the leatherworking ones were not, and I could use the extra income to bolster me while I figured my shit out. Mom, Sadie, and Henry looked at me like I was insane. Gramps smiled, those features softening. Logan though—I think I'd pretty much broken him. He opened his mouth, then shut it, then opened it again.

"Sweetie, you already work two jobs," Mom said, placing a hand on my shoulder. She offered me this look filled with so much awe that I couldn't stand it, like I was some huge success and not floundering.

"It's the slow season for leatherworking," I lied, not wanting to admit my business was perpetually slow.

"Do you even read?" Logan said, which had my jaw clenching all over again.

"No, I'm illiterate," I deadpanned. He'd spent years making his low opinion of me clear, but for fuck's sake, I'd grown up with Gramps's love of books around me. Even if my tastes weren't whatever highbrow literary bullshit he probably read, I liked a good thriller as much as anyone.

"That's not what I meant," he said, waving his hand. "I just meant are you going to want to recommend books to the customers and such? They're a demanding bunch."

"Coop spent a summer working at the store back in high school," Gramps interrupted. "He knows how things are done."

My chest warmed with pride at Gramps coming to my defense, and Logan took the cue and shut his infuriating mouth, even though he kept passing me furtive looks. Most likely plotting a murder by glitter bomb or something equally annoying. Which—why had I agreed to this again? Oh yeah, because I loved my family, and I could use the cash.

"Well then," he said, throwing his aggravating smile my way. "Get ready to see a whole lot more of me."

Hell. I was going to be in hell.

Chapter Four

Logan

The "open" sign flipped over for Fox's Restaurant, and I all but bolted out of my car.

Coop hadn't showed up yet, though he'd be here on time, despite hating mornings. The man was incapable of being late, but I wanted to ride my morning-person advantage here and arrive fifteen minutes before our set meeting. Honestly though, seven thirty wasn't that early. The man was a big baby—evidenced by the way he freaked out over harmless pranks.

I tugged at the pale blue button-down I wore with the sleeves rolled up. When I walked past the windows of the restaurant along the walkway, I caught a glimpse of my styled hair, tempted to tweak it again. This wasn't a date. Furthest thing from, so I didn't know why I'd bothered with the Armani aftershave and my fuck-me jeans when I'd gotten ready.

Most likely because I'd jerked off last night over the thought of spending shifts with him up close and personal. Coop working at the bookstore was a fantasy of mine. Not the work part, but hell, the only time I managed to get his eyes on me was when I pissed him off. So, I'd continued to do it from high school onward until, ten years later, we were still circling one another.

My hand settled onto the handle of the door. Maybe today would be the start of something different.

I licked my lips as I tugged the door open. Probably not.

The scent of coffee percolating reached me at once, and I sucked in a deep inhale, the smell settling deep in my bones. I'd die without my steady caffeine fix. Not for the wake-up in the morning but as fuel for my perky ass and attitude.

Fox's Restaurant was a staple here, all wooden beam ceilings, paste-white walls, and tons of windows inviting the sunlight inside. The four-seater circular tables were stationed in the middle of the place, but all the beige booths lined the sides, which I gunned for. I caught sight of Mae behind the open kitchen section to the far right.

"You beat Mrs. Davison here," Mae called out. "She's going to be pissed."

"Tell her to hustle a little faster then," I said, striding to the back booth I always chose.

"I'll leave that to you," Mae responded. "I value my life."

As much as I wanted to take advantage of having some one-on-one time with Cooper Ellis, we did need to go through our work arrangement for Gramps's shop. The old man liked to pretend he'd be hustling around town in a matter of a week, but a break like his would take a smidge longer to heal.

And idiot me, I'd just agreed to an interview with the remote company.

It wasn't for another two weeks, but Gramps wouldn't be magically better by then. We were looking at a month at least until he could handle a shift on his own, which would make him more ornery than a fox in a cage. That man hated sitting around idle.

I slid into the booth, the vinyl giving a slight creak with the motion. The door swung open, and Mrs. Davison strode in, wearing her flannel shirt tucked into her jeans like she'd been doing her entire life—or at least for as long as I'd been alive. Said it showed off her belt buckle better or some shit. Woman was in her seventies but with more energy than I had most days.

"Logan, what the hell are you doing here so early?" Her voice boomed across the room.

"And good morning to you too," I called, resisting the urge to straighten up.

"Aren't kids your age still sleeping the day away?" she continued as she headed to her normal booth, thankfully on the opposite end of the room as me.

"Considering I'm nearing thirty, I don't think I qualify for kid status anymore." I snagged the plastic menu to give myself something to flip through.

"I'll be the judge of that," she said.

Mae ignored the whole conversation, which she was a pro at doing, and I debated getting into an argument with Mrs. Davison that would go into roundabouts. But honestly, I was pretty sick of the older folks around town viewing me as the snot-nosed little shit I'd been in high school. I got launched into adulthood the moment Mom passed.

Before I could bring up the statistics on my side, not hers, the door swung open again.

Cooper Ellis stepped in with a scowl, but it softened when he caught Mae's eyes on him. Asshole knew how to play the game, which was why everyone around town loved him while I was just the joke. He leaned into grunts and brooding quiet in the morning, which gave him the vibe of a steady, quiet guy, not the firebrand I liked to provoke.

Both versions were equally hot though.

He nodded to Mae before heading in my direction. I leaned back in the booth as I watched him approach, taking a moment to appreciate the view. His tan skin had nicks and marks along his arms from the type of work he did, but it was smooth around the face, the dark scruff accenting his strong chin, dimple and all. His eyes were the intense sort of blue that reminded me of the lakes around here in the spring, and he all but pinned me with his gaze.

His powerful muscles flexed with his stride, the white tank and open red flannel showcasing them well. His jeans were weathered from use, tucked into steel-toed boots, which made a solid sound with every heavy step in my direction.

A grin lifted my lips unbidden.

"You look fresh and sparkling this morning," I called out, not bothering to hide my glee. While, yes, this might be a chance to get him to take me seriously, I also couldn't help the compulsion to needle him that leapt to the fore whenever he scowled my way. Was I continuing my own problem here? Well, sure, but I'd always been the master of self-sabotage.

"Whose idea was it to meet before eight in the morning?" Coop grumbled as he slung himself into the seat opposite me. The scent of metal and leather overwhelmed me at once, activating my drool reflex the way it always had. Coop had been working around leather since he was a teen though, so the two were always entwined in my brain. Maybe explained my fixation with certain other leather implements.

"I'm just being sensible," I responded with a sniff as I cracked open the menu. "We both have businesses to get to and plus, breakfast."

Coop scrubbed his palms across his face. "Why did I agree to this again?"

"Clearly because your ego needed the boost of swooping in as the hero yet again." I flicked my gaze over the top of the menu. "Or because you secretly looove me and want to spend all this time together."

"Well, that's not fucking it," Coop muttered.

I ignored the small pang of disappointment that flared in my chest because a sliver of me still hoped one day Cooper Ellis would look at me with something other than disgust. However, I had known our ship was sunk from the moment I "stole" his girlfriend in high school. Penny was a raging lesbian, and I was a raging homosexual, and we decided to be a ragingly awesome fake couple until the end of high school. Neither of us had been ready to come out at the time.

"Okay, first things first, food," I said, spotting Mae with her slow approach in our direction. Her pink-framed glasses stood out from here, along with the pink Crocs she wore.

Coop licked his lips and stared at the menu. "You order first. I'll catch up."

I rolled my eyes. As if he didn't get the same thing for breakfast every time.

"All right, boys," Mae said, stepping up with her notepad in hand. "What'll it be today?"

"Breakfast wrap for me, plus two coffees," I said with a flutter of my lashes. "And biscuits and gravy for Coop here."

Coop's head jerked up. "No one asked you to order for me."

"Oh, so you're not going to get that?" I asked, arching an eyebrow.

Mae snorted. "He's not wrong, Coop. Any time you make it out for breakfast, you always ask for the same thing."

Coop sucked in a sharp breath before flashing Mae a smile, like he hadn't just been glowering at me. "Sounds good."

Mae clicked her pen as she jotted down her notes, then sashayed back to the open kitchen to get started on our order.

"Please don't tell me you're paying attention to what I eat so you can slip laxatives into my food." Coop massaged his temples, chugging full steam ahead on the Irritation Train. "You haven't done food pranks yet by some miracle, but I can assume they're on your agenda at some point."

"You act like I plan these on a weekly basis," I responded, fiddling with one of the napkins at the table. "The odd prank once in a while hardly warrants the amount of grumpiness you sling at me every time I see you."

"My existence hardly warrants the amount of shit you've done to me over the years," Coop countered. "Stealing my girlfriend—"

"Ah, that old chestnut," I interrupted, earning another dirty glare from him. The more annoyed he got though, the more intense his eyes became, and I had to wonder if he looked like that during sex. The man had growly Dom written all over him—though that was probably wishful thinking on my part.

"Sabotaging my dates? Denting my car? Look, even yesterday, what inspired vandalizing my storefront?" Coop was getting the jaw twitch I loved to see, as if he bubbled up with steam and needed somewhere to vent.

I leaned my arms along the back of the booth. "Vandalizing is a very strong word for a friendly sign. I was just trying to drum up business. The place looked pretty dead."

Coop's eyes locked on mine, sudden thunderstorms charging in them. "Fuck off, Logan."

My brows drew together. There was something a bit more serious in his tone there, nothing like the normal replies he gave me.

"Well, before I do that, we've got a schedule to hash out and some breakfast to eat," I said, tilting my head toward the kitchen. Mae approached with two mugs of coffee, and I welcomed the distraction to cut the awkward tension in the air.

She plunked them down in front of us. "I'll be right back with your food too."

"Thanks, love," I responded, and she rolled her eyes at me, even though her lips curled in a smile.

I poured a hefty amount of sugar into my coffee and a few creamers to make it delicious while Mr. Someone Pissed in My Cornflakes swallowed a gulp black.

"Don't want to sweeten it up at all? A little bit of sugar might do wonders for your personality."

Coop glowered back. "Everyone else seems to like my personality just fine."

"Lucky for you, I enjoy being special," I responded as I took a sip from my mug. I turned on the screen to my phone and flipped to my Google Calendar. "Right now, Gramps and I overlap on a lot of the shifts, since the bookstore is only open from ten to six. I work the full length from Sunday to Thursday, and Gramps takes Friday and Saturday on top of whenever else he wants to come in. That changes around a bit based on the week, but we can keep a rigid schedule to work with yours."

Coop stared at me like I was speaking in tongues.

"Have any questions?" I asked, taking another sip from my deliciously sweet coffee. The creamy liquid trickled down my throat.

"No, I just think that was the longest I've ever heard you talk seriously about something," Coop responded, rubbing his thumb across the surface of his mug. Fuck, his weathered hands were like porn for me, all rough and callused.

"Just because you don't inspire it doesn't mean I'm not capable," I shot back, right in time for Mae to swing over with our breakfasts. As always, Fox's portions were out of control. I would probably only eat half of my breakfast burrito while Coop would inhale his entire plate. Given I was half a foot shorter than him, I guess he needed to get the extra calories in.

"I can take Saturdays," Coop said, "but I can't do the full Friday shift. I could do half days with you on Thursdays and Fridays though?"

"Works for me. You can come in later this week, and I'll run you through the system." I chewed a bite of the breakfast burrito, restraining my happy sigh. Something about the hash browns, eggs, and cheese mixed together with the bacon and peppers worked for me every time. The urge to keep poking at Coop surged up in a real way, mostly because this quiet between us wasn't what I'd grown used to. It also made me even more aware of my attraction to him that had never died.

Truth be told, I'd rather he hate me a little than see genuine resignation in his eyes when he shut me down.

"It shouldn't be for too long," I said to break the silence. Cooper continued chewing on the biscuits and gravy that he acted like he didn't need all while fixing me with his steady stare. "Your grandfather should be able to get back on the floor in a few weeks."

Coop swallowed his food, his Adam's apple bobbing. "Not you too. Gramps is going to be trying to return to work far earlier than he should."

"I'm not recommending he be climbing any bookshelves—he can leave a pile for reshelving for me at the end of his shifts," I said. "But you and I both know keeping him cooped up for long stints will drive him to dangerous lengths. I wouldn't be surprised if you found him learning to hotwire cars and break safes with all his spare time."

A genuine laugh escaped Coop, one that lit his features, his eyes crinkling at the sides. Fuck, that was rare. My insides glowed.

"If you're implying Gramps might start a thieving ring in Collier's Creek, you're probably right."

Coop finished the last bits of the food on his plate, licking the tines of his fork. I tried not to bite my lip and stare too long at the way he lapped at the utensil, because holy hell, that was making me hard.

I shifted in my seat and nearly inhaled my mug of coffee at this point. This whole "getting along in close proximity" thing was hazardous to my heart. And my poor neglected sex life.

"Are you sure you're not going to burn yourself out?" I asked again. Coop's swooping in to save the day with his family knew no bounds, and while most didn't take advantage, I could see how much it wore on him.

He offered an attempt at a smile that failed. "Slow season for the leather shop, so don't sweat it." The storm returned to his eyes.

Maybe it was because I'd been watching him for years, but whatever had bothered him earlier, it had to do with the shop. Lucky for me, I had weeks ahead of close contact from working at the bookshop together to extract the information.

In the meanwhile, I'd need to get laid fast.

Because all this time spent with Cooper Ellis was pushing me close to detonation.

Chapter Five

Cooper

Ellis Books looked the same as it had my entire life.

The black lettering overlaid the painted pale green sign over the store, and glass covered the front, letting everyone see the stacks and stacks of books that waited for them inside. While I'd been in bookstores that were truly junk heaps filled with teetering piles and I'd visited the big box ones where everything felt pin-perfect and a little too neat, Gramps's store was the middle ground.

Gramps had arrived home yesterday, and already, he was "forgetting" his crutches when he needed to get something from the other room, and my mom and dad were about to strap him to his recliner.

I pushed the door open, and the scent of vanilla from the lignin and leather from the bindings greeted my nose. Old books had a special place in my heart from Gramps alone, but he made sure to have variety in his store, including newer releases as well. Leaving Ellis Leatherworking this morning had pained me, mostly because a part of me that worried I'd miss out on a potential order if I wasn't there—even if the walk-ins came few and far between with my line of work.

My gaze skimmed past the dozens of bookshelves filled with adventures to the desk at the side of the store, the same one Gramps always sat behind. The old-timey cash register was gone, so I did have to learn a few different tricks with how Gramps and Logan operated, but apart from the books they stocked, the rest of the store hadn't changed much over the years.

Logan sat behind the desk today, his laptop pulled out. He hunched forward, a serious expression on his face, which was a rarity in and of itself. When he wasn't opening his mouth to lob obnoxiousness my way, I couldn't just ignore how pretty he was. Pouty lips, those deep-set eyes, and thick, tousled blond hair the perfect length to tug. Inconvenient lust coursed through me, accelerating the thump, thump, thump in my chest.

I'd always found him attractive though, in the rare moments he wasn't doing something to piss me off.

"Reporting for duty," I announced myself as I strode farther into the store. Reaching out to the shelves, I skimmed my fingertips along the spines of the books while I walked closer.

Logan looked up at me and licked his lips, highlighting his often-infuriating but damn enticing mouth. "Punctual as always."

"You say that like there's something wrong with being on time." I crossed my arms as I came to a stop in front of the desk.

"Would it kill you to fuck up with something for once?" Logan leaned back in his seat, arching a brow. Familiar irritation began to prickle across my chest. "Mr. Varsity Football, Collier King in the Jake Day festival, all-around upstanding citizen."

Logan kept going, and the urge to smack something, preferably him, kept rising. The asshole had no idea the crushing weight I shouldered every damn day—with my business, with my family, and with the community just to keep everyone happy. If I dropped the ball, people noticed. I couldn't mouth off and charm my way out of situations like him. And little did Logan know, I was already fucking up big-time with my business. No matter how I advertised, the different strategies I tried around town, nothing had worked to revitalize my flagging leatherwork shop.

"For a second there, I thought we would have a civil shift together," I muttered. "Clearly, that was a passing daydream." Fuck, I needed more than a single coffee to get through this day.

"I have no idea what you're talking about," Logan said, slapping his palms against the surface of the desk. "I'm perfectly peachy."

"You always are," I responded. He licked his lips again, and the slight flush that dusted his cheeks when he glanced to me, his eyes sharp, made me realize the other connotation of the phrase.

Because yeah, his ass was perfectly peach shaped. If I had to suffer through him torturing me, at least I could appreciate the spectacular view.

"Okay, so to ring customers up," Logan said, switching directions at a whiplash pace like he always did. Either he was avoidant, couldn't stay on task, or both. He lifted a tablet and fixed it in place. "I forced your grandfather to update to modern times, so we're not using the hunk of metal that resided here when I started."

"I don't know, the old cash register wasn't so hard to figure out," I drawled, giving Logan a little bit of pushback.

Logan fixed me with a dramatic glare. "It took me six full months to sway him to just let me try. Don't you dare put that back out there."

I nodded at the tablet, the screen on with the interface showing. "I use the same type at Ellis Leatherworking, so that'll be a breeze. And I assume the rest of it hasn't changed? Helping customers, reshelving books, ordering new stock?"

"How dare you reduce my complicated job to such simplistic terms," Logan said, plastering a hand across his chest. "I'll have you know, those book clubs don't organize themselves, and forcing Gramps into modern marketing has been a Herculean effort. He interrupted ten attempts in a row at filming an Instagram reel so he could wave at the camera."

A snort escaped me even though I wanted to bite it back, because I could imagine Gramps eager to be a part of whatever Logan tried to do. "What are you attempting with popping this place up on Instagram? It's not like most of this town doesn't already know Ellis Books is here."

Logan shot me a look. "Oh, so it's all Ellis men who are terrible at marketing, not just your grandfather. Come on, who wouldn't want to cash in on all the tourist money? Not just that—with the ability to order shit online, you've got to compete for people's attention. Give them a reason to stroll on down to your shop and pick up the book they've been eyeing rather than one-clicking on Amazon."

Embarrassment rushed through me. I hadn't thought about any of the marketing that way. I was trash at social media, so I hadn't gone hard into setting up pages for my job, but I hated to admit Logan was making a lot of sense. Begrudging respect welled up inside me, along with the realization that maybe I'd only been seeing one aspect of the man for all these years.

"So, what are you doing working here with all your marketing know-how?" I asked. Truth be told, I wasn't even sure what Logan had gone to college for. He'd stayed local, even though he hadn't been around as much five years back. Then he'd reappeared and started working with Gramps, and his infiltration into my family had begun.

Logan's brows drew together, and his expression darkened for a moment before he pasted a grin on his face. "Excuse me, who wouldn't want to be surrounded by books every day? Living the dream here." He paused to give me a deadpan look. "I guess not everyone would appreciate a bookstore though. Should I put you in the high school required reading section?"

I shook my head in disbelief. Every time I thought he might have more depth, the asshole pivoted and made me want to strangle him instead. "I've read books past high school."

"Trade books for work don't count," Logan said, pointing a finger my way.

I shifted my hips, needing to move something so I didn't lunge across the desk.

The front door tinkled, signaling a customer's arrival.

Thank fuck. Any longer standing around and talking to Logan and I wasn't sure what I might do.

"Ooh, think of this as a test run," Logan said, leaning forward in his seat. He rested his elbows on the desk and looked up at me. "Go get 'em, killer."

I clenched my jaw again and sucked in a sharp breath as I focused on the customer. Max Stone wandered in, the silver fox investor who'd swept into town and won over Nash. He cracked a smile as I approached, lifting a hand in welcome.

"You're working here now too?" he asked.

I shook my head. Since he was from out of town, he wasn't as in on the pulse of all the gossip as the rest of us. On the way here, at least seven folks in town had stopped me to offer sympathies for Gramps and his broken leg. He'd apparently taken Logan's idea of claiming he'd injured himself on the rolling ladders in a *Beauty and the Beast* recreation. "Gramps broke his leg, so I'm filling in for a little bit."

"This is his first day, so make him work hard," Logan called out, his irritating voice one I would hear in my nightmares tonight.

"I just wanted to poke around the used books, so unfortunately you won't get much of a challenge here," Max said, offering a grin. "Hope your Gramps heals up soon."

"Thanks, man." I hooked a thumb in my jeans pocket. Clearly, I'd be fine running the place on my own.

"Boo, boo," Logan called over from the desk he was glued to. "We need a Mr. Norris level challenge."

My nose wrinkled as I settled into a lean on the side of the desk. "Let me guess, obscure World War II books?"

"Clearly," Logan said with an eyeroll. "It's all the man adores. However, he stands behind you and breathes heavily when you look things up, and it's almost as excruciating as the tangents he goes into when he's trying to explain what book he's searching for."

"Come on, Mr. Well-Rounded Book Nerd," I shot back. "Are you book shaming him?"

Logan shot me a look. "No. I'm shaming social etiquette."

I crossed my arms, a smirk twitching at my lips. "Oh, you're one to criticize social niceties."

"Niceties and etiquette are two separate things," Logan responded, those dark brown eyes flaring with amusement. "Though you'd know that if you read more."

I let out a slow exhale through my clenched teeth to keep myself from reaching over and wringing Logan's neck. He watched me cheekily, clearly soaking up my irritation like he always did. My fuse for most folks tended to be longer than average, but something about this guy just set me to sparks every time.

"Oh, since you'll be here over the next few weeks, I'll need your help with the book crates too," Logan said, still typing away at his laptop. Curiosity overcame me, and I peeked over his shoulder.

"God, what are you, Mr. Norris? Stop breathing in my ear." He swatted back and lightly smacked me on the cheek. The quick brush sent a bolt through me, like I'd gotten static-shocked. Not like it mattered—I'd caught a glimpse of what he'd been working on. The book crates he referred to. A full color-coded spreadsheet had been up with names, addresses, book names, the whole gamut.

"So, you've got Gramps doing social media and book crates now? How did you pull off this witchcraft?" Envy shot through me. If I had half of Logan's savvy, my business wouldn't be tanking as hard as it was. He'd kept Ellis Books afloat when it easily could've shut down, and it was clear from the brief scan I'd done around the place that his new ideas were everywhere. Plus, I heard about them—the cheese and wine nights, the book clubs, all of the stuff he'd arranged once he started here.

Not like anyone wanted to do a cheese and wine night at a leather-working studio, but maybe I needed to think outside the box.

Logan shrugged. "He lets me have fun. This is the part I love about running a business—the marketing end of things, and working with books? Even better. Not like my freelance editing work is going to pay the bills."

"You edit too?" I asked. Considering how long we'd known each other for, it shocked me how little I'd learned about Logan. Maybe because his constant pranks and mouthy comments pushed me away every time, but still, I should've been more aware.

"Just the occasional freelance job here and there," he said. "It's what I got my degree for, right?"

The edge to his voice sounded unlike the flippant tone I normally received, but before I could hone in, the door swung open again.

This time, Kai strode inside. Considering he was more likely to dive into a video game than a book in his free time, he'd arrived to bother me. My dumbass had made the mistake of telling him I was starting here today.

"Don't you have a job to be at?" I called over to Kai.

He cracked a grin, his pale green eyes crinkling. "Logan, you better tell Gramps that Coop here doesn't know how to greet customers."

"Duly noted," Logan said, a fox-like grin curling his lips. I restrained an eye roll. Like Logan needed more fodder to torment me with.

"What brought you this way?" I asked, clapping a hand on Kai's shoulder when he got within range. We were as close as could be, but I wasn't the hugging sort. My siblings had wrung them from me when they were younger, but the same puppy eyes didn't work now.

"I've got the order from Wild Crest Ranch," Kai said, plucking out a yellow piece of paper.

Relief settled in my bones, and my shoulders relaxed on instinct. This should be enough to keep me afloat for another month, but by no means would it work as a long-term plan.

"I tried to poke around to see if they were looking to replace their usual guy, but it sounds like this is one and done." Kai wrinkled his nose as he passed over the paper. "Sorry."

Logan's gaze burned into me from the side, and I tried to ignore it as embarrassment heated my cheeks. The last thing I needed was Logan Nichols finding out my business was in trouble. He'd spread word around town and would probably help set the shop itself on fire.

"You searching for more clientele?" Logan asked, and my shoulders tensed. When I glanced his way, there wasn't a mocking look in his eyes for once, but hell, I couldn't even tell my family what I was going through. There was no way I would confess to the guy who'd made it his life's mission to torment me for God knows what reason.

"Like I said, slow season." I dragged my gaze away from Logan and back to Kai, who fixed me with an arched brow. Assholes everywhere.

"Mind if I grab this?" Max said as he approached, breaking through the awkward tension. Oh thank fuck. He lifted up a worn copy of *The Hobbit*.

"Let me ring you up," I said, snagging the tablet. I should've looked over the interface a bit more, but it was easier to sort through than my own, even with the amount of inventory. Seriously, how was Logan so talented at all of this? We were the same damn age. Within seconds, I had the sale set up and the card reader plugged in.

"Look at how hard he's concentrating," Kai said in a stage whisper.

"Technology's *so* difficult," Logan responded. "All that pushing-buttons nonsense. Easy-to-read screens are just the worst."

Max snorted while the pair of them continued jabbering back and forth, and I clenched my jaw as I ran his card. Kai and Logan in the same room meant bad news for me. I never realized similarities between them in the past, but with the way they were both needling me—apparently I attracted impish little shits.

"Sign here, and you're all good," I said, handing the card and the tablet over to Max.

"You made it through," Logan teased, wiping a hand over his forehead. "It was touch and go for a few moments there."

"Keep up that pace, and you're likely to help three whole customers on each shift." Kai jumped in too.

Max shook his head with a grin. "Thanks for the book, guys. I'll see you all around." With that, he headed back toward the door, and I wanted to beg him to take me with him.

"See, the furrow there means he's pissed." Kai pointed at my brow.

"I'm *well* familiar with that one," Logan responded, a twinkle in his dark eyes.

I scrubbed my palms against my face.

This was going to be one long-as-fuck day.

Chapter Six

Logan

Thank fuck for later opening hours.

Coop had started last week, and, predictably, being around him all day had ended in an epic session with my hand later that night. Not like I got off a ton at home—staying at Aunt Beth's house put a damper on my masturbation. Maybe for the better, otherwise the surfaces of my place might be covered in jizz. Based on the amount of financial stress I was under, masturbating or getting fucked should've been a top priority for relief. At least I could hook up steadily enough to slake my thirst, even though I rarely got to scratch my itch for a little more kink in the bedroom.

I tweaked my styled hair, staring at it in my laptop's screen. Remote work meant remote interview, and since they started at seven in the morning, they were fine with a nine a.m. interview, which left me time to scoot over to Ellis Books to begin my shift. I chewed on the inside of my cheek, ignoring the weight of the guilt settling over my shoulders.

I'd visited Gramps at home the other day. He was going out of his mind there, but the gratitude he'd heaped on me had made me feel worse. The relationship I'd developed with him was one of my closest, and going on this interview meant betraying him. He'd mentioned having me take over the business when he eventually retired too, and part of me longed to do that. If I didn't have Mom's cancer bills that dumbass me had cosigned on, I'd be happy as anything splitting my time running a bookstore and editing. Honestly, that combo was everything I'd hoped to do.

However, I was getting close to thirty and didn't want to still be living with my aunt either.

A loud squawk dragged me back to the present. Jim Squawkins was in fine form today, picking at his pinfeathers and strutting around his cage and preening. A cream white parrot with a yellow pouf on his head, the guy was completely ridiculous.

I stared at the video call, seeing myself in the screen while I waited for them to join on. I looked miserable as shit, which wouldn't get me the job. Maybe if I thought of the last book I read—nope, wait, that had tentacles in some very sexy places. I chewed on my lower lip. Getting a boner for my interview wasn't my best idea either. Only thing that would make it worse was to have Coop burst into my room—naked.

My cock hardened at the thought, pushing against the fabric of the pajama pants I hid under the screen cutoff.

"Hi, Logan?" a voice sounded. I looked up. The interviewer was an older woman, her grays tucked into a neat bun and wearing a prim shade of magenta lipstick.

Well, shit.

"Uh, hi," I said, hoping I didn't sound too high-pitched there. Not every day you push through an interview with an erection. Thank fuck this wasn't in person.

Squawwwwwk.

"What was that?" she asked, and I internally groaned.

"My parrot," I clarified as Jim let out another hearty noise.

"Ah, cute. I'm glad we're able to talk," she continued, leading the charge. I listened as she extolled the virtues of the company, and I bobbed my head in intervals and made the requisite "mmm" noises. My erection listened intently as well, refusing to deflate, even as I tried to push at it—that clearly didn't help.

"Tell me a little bit about yourself," she said, throwing stock line after stock line.

I forced a grin. Obviously, she didn't want to know about inconvenient boners. Time to tuck it away and pull my charm out.

Squawwwk.

Jim interrupted right as I opened my mouth.

Today was off to a great start.

After a whole shift at Ellis's Books shouldering the guilt of the interview I'd had in the morning, I needed a drink. Or a dozen.

The company wanted me to go through one more round of interviews, which seemed ridiculous, but they were definitely interested. Even if I wasn't. For fuck's sake, watching Jim Squawkins pick at his molting feathers sounded better than entering information into a database forty hours a week. But the salary would be enough that I could move out of Aunt Beth's, even with all the shitty bills hanging over my head.

My gut sat sour as I approached Jake's Tap in the center of town. The yellow neons spelled out the name, brighter from the encroaching shadows. The sun was setting but not the glorious reds and golds we usually witnessed out here—no, today was as murky and gray as my mood. Already, a few folks hung around the front of the building sharing a smoke, including old man Kinsey, who had a permanent spot at the bar—to the point they'd written his name on his stool.

There were a few other bars in town, but they got flooded by out-of-towners, whereas this was *the* townie bar. Anyone who lived here year-round preferred to meet up here, unless they wanted to score with someone new.

When I stepped in, the smell of hops and cedar hit me full force, and I drank it in. The lights weren't overly bright, all burnished brass fixtures, and the floor glowed from a solid polishing—which was good, since it wouldn't look nearly as pretty by the end of the night. The folks around here knew how to drink as readily as they knew how to gossip.

Drew was working behind the counter, his simple black tee highlighting his broad shoulders and trim waist. We'd hooked up once upon a time, but seeing as both of us preferred bottoming to topping, our sexual compatibility hadn't been fireworks. Still, we got along great. I headed straight for the big cedar bar with the gleaming counter. The barstools were red vinyl and mostly occupied, but I found two seats so I could save one for Penny.

The booths were starting to fill up too, more red vinyl seats and wooden tables, with a level of privacy more suited to going on a date or a quiet hang with friends. I was looking for enough noise to block out my guilt tonight, so the bar it was.

"We've got Collier's Pale Ale on tap," Drew said, grabbing a glass as he met my gaze.

"Fill 'er up." I settled into the worn barstool and slumped forward. My skin simmered, mostly from pent-up tension at more encounters than normal with Coop. While we weren't sharing shifts like the first day, we had overlap two days of the week, and all that time around his rumbling voice and the strong scent of leather had me horny as fuck.

Maybe I should've gone to one of the other bars.

Drew passed the pint over, and when I grasped it, the coolness of the glass imprinted on my palm. An audible sigh slipped from my lips.

"You okay, Logan?" Drew asked, stopping to idle.

Normally, I'd love the chance to vent, but this situation wasn't one I wanted to spread either. If I got the job, I hadn't decided if I would take it or not, but the promise of having my own place, of not worrying over every cent I spent was a lure.

"Just exhausted with Gramps out for a spell," I said, plastering on a false smile.

"I heard Cooper's stepping in for him?" Drew asked, his dark eyes gleaming. "How's that been?"

I rolled my eyes. Most of the town had sussed out my crush on Coop years ago. The only two people who remained oblivious were Penny and Coop himself, even when everyone told the two of them to their faces. "Terrible," I responded. "He's grumpy as fuck and glares at me whenever we have to be in the same room together."

"So, business as usual." Drew laughed as he glanced over to the opposite end of the bar. Rye Levine, the owner, had showed up, which wasn't much of a surprise—the guy hung around most nights. With his curly auburn hair and green eyes, he was definitely a stunner. "Boss is here," Drew said, drifting in the direction of Rye. "I'm going to go catch up real fast."

I tipped my head in a nod before taking the first sip of my beer. The refreshing liquid coursed down my throat, and I savored the temporary moment of relief it brought me. I'd have to nurse this one because until payday hit, I couldn't afford to spend too much on incidentals.

The door swung open, and my gaze drifted toward it. Penny bounced in, her red waves of hair all but trailing behind her with how fast she moved.

"Did something catch on fire?" I asked when she came to a halt in front of me.

Penny flung herself into the seat and scrubbed at her face. I sat up a little taller and paid attention. Whatever was going on with her probably offered a much better distraction. "A gorgeous fucking girl called me beautiful on the way here. Asked what I was up to—if I wanted to meet her at the bar."

"Okay," I said, taking another sip of my beer.

"She asked for my number, and I froze. Was this supposed to be a friend thing? Was she hitting on me? So, instead of giving her my number, I tossed out some awkward-as-fuck finger guns and was like 'Maybe I'll see you there.'" She slumped over the bar, pressing her forehead against the surface.

A laugh exploded from me, loud enough to draw a few glances. "Like the freaking Fonz? What did you do after that?"

"Ran here," she muttered, the sound muffled with her face toward the counter.

Amusement bubbled up in my gut, the exact medicine for my conflicted mind. I swear, I'd never met a person worse at picking up signals. "Did you want more with her?"

"Not now," Penny continued. "I ruined it."

I shook my head, my grin still twitching my lips even as my laughter died down. "Penny, I don't know how to explain this more clearly—if she's calling you beautiful and asking for your number, she's hitting on you."

"Or I misread the whole thing," she said, lifting her head. "Maybe she just wanted a friend."

Lordy, not this again. "Why don't you have a drink and think it over really hard."

Penny's eyes narrowed. "Don't take that patronizing tone with me, Logan Michael Nichols."

"Hey." A husky voice came from behind us. I glanced back to spot a woman standing there, her arms crossed and a smirk on her lips. She was Penny's type to a T—tattooed and wearing a red flannel with the sleeves rolled up to her elbows, which showcased some serious forearms. Her dark brown hair was pulled into a ponytail, and the amusement on her face spelled good news for Penny.

Penny turned around to face her, cringing when she realized who it was.

"You know," the chick said, "we could've just walked here together."

"Not after I acted like a complete weirdo," Penny muttered.

"She's impossible at reading signs," I offered, and Tattooed Chick's grin widened.

"I'm seeing that," Tattooed Chick responded before switching her focus to Penny. "I'll go nab one of the corner tables. If you'd like to join me, I'll be waiting right there. If not, no sweat."

With that, she swaggered on over to the aforementioned table. My chest squeezed tight. So much for getting to vent to my bestie. Penny was about the only person I felt comfortable telling all this crap to, but I also didn't want to hold her back. Because she was definitely glued the entire time Tattooed Chick sauntered to the seat.

"Go over there," I said, tugging at her sleeve.

Penny wrinkled her nose. "I came here to hang with you though."

"Which we can do tomorrow. I'm here enjoying my beer, and there are plenty of folks I can talk to. That hottie wants you, and it's clear you're interested in her too." I wanted to scream "don't leave me" but I was only mid-tier clingy. At least one of us would have the chance to get laid tonight. Maybe I could jerk off in the bathroom for thrills.

"You're the best," she said, hopping up from her seat. She leaned in and pressed a kiss to my temple. "Do I look okay?"

"Gorgeous," I said. "Now, go get her."

Penny flounced over in the direction of Tattooed Chick, and the feline smile the woman gave her upon approach confirmed everything I'd been saying. However, now I needed to figure out what to do with my night. Chances were, I wouldn't find a one-night stand here, which meant if I wanted to get dicked down, the other bar would be a better bet. My legs felt like lead though, which was making paying up and peeling myself away difficult.

I glared at my half-drunk pint, refusing to leave without finishing this one first.

"What pissed you off?" Rye asked, settling into the seat beside me.

"The ending of *Game of Thrones*, but that's a long discussion you don't have the time for," I responded, not wanting to dive into my issues. The whole point of coming out here had been a distraction, but all these nosy, caring, also still nosy people loved to check in on everyone, and apparently I was putting out vibes.

"I heard your three-hour rant the day after it aired," Rye said, waving a hand. "More information than I ever needed on the show."

"I could rant about the books if you'd like," I continued. "Since, you know—"

"They'll never get finished." Rye completed the sentence for me, an amused grin on his lips.

I sniffed loudly. "Look, there are some topics worth revisiting." The door swung open again with a creak, and I couldn't help but glance in the direction.

Coop strode in, looking hot as hell in a gray Henley that hugged his muscles in all the right places and some tighter Wranglers, free from holes for once. My body was suddenly paying attention, the prickle of awareness enhancing all the confusing shit buzzing in my brain today.

The reason for Coop's put-together appearance strode in right after him, a pretty brunette who was definitely not a local.

My heart sank. Of course. Coop was here on a date.

I glanced at my beer and then back in the direction Coop headed, toward a four-seater table.

Couldn't hurt to go over and introduce myself. After all, I still had a beer to finish.

Chapter Seven

Cooper

I'd been on edge for most of the week. Maybe a little because I'd completed the order from Wild Crest and they didn't want more work at the time. Maybe a lot because my usual Logan interactions had been dialed up to eleven. The man lived to annoy me, but what made it worse was that the increased dosage as of late had me noticing his perky ass more and more. Or those pouty lips and how good they looked wrapped around the end of the pen he liked to suck on while he worked.

How good they'd look wrapped around my cock.

The obvious solution was to hop onto my dating profile, find a match with an out-of-towner, and throw myself into whatever distraction I could find.

Daria had met me outside Jake's Tap, our local watering hole. She was petite, with glossy chestnut waves, gorgeous deep-set eyes, and definite curves, but my libido hadn't started sparking from mere sight. Maybe I could've taken her to the other bar, but this one was familiar, and I liked it. Kinsey offered a wave as we headed to the entrance, deep in conversation with a few of the other older guys in town. I nodded back.

"Is this the place with all the local charm?" Daria asked as we stepped inside.

I zeroed in on the open back tables, where I preferred to take dates. Last thing I wanted was for us to be in broad sight at the bar where my siblings would most likely stop by and interrupt every five seconds. I'd already gotten seven messages from Sadie about her decision to take in a wounded pocket gopher and four from Henry to complain about Mom stealing all the tomatoes from his garden.

"Charm's a bit of a stretch," I said, going for honesty. "But you can get a good beer here, and it's not overly loud."

"Ah, a quiet guy," Daria said, flashing me an entertained grin. She was the right sort of pretty that should've had my brain thinking bedroom, but apparently my brain was broken. I blamed the menace I temporarily worked with at Ellis Books, because he kept appearing in all my fantasies as of late.

"Yeah, that's my preference," I responded, pulling out a seat for her. She slid into place while I settled across from her, ready to focus on dinner and the gorgeous woman in front of me.

"You'd hate my type of job then," Daria said, popping the menu open and giving it a scan. "I'm a pharmaceutical rep, so I'm constantly talking with new people—in the area for the weekend."

"I'm used to chatter," I responded. "Just don't need to contribute much of it myself."

"What would you recommend here?" she asked as she skimmed over the menu. "I'm assuming it's all cowboy type of food?"

I arched a brow. "And what would cowboy food entail?"

"Meat, meat, and more meat." Her coy, flirty tone would've normally drawn my interest, but nada.

"Did somebody say meat?" an all-too-familiar voice called out. I withheld my groan. Of course. The exact person I was trying to avoid right now. My pulse picked up, mostly because I wanted to strangle Logan from mere words alone. I refused to acknowledge the other reason why it elevated.

The seat adjacent to Daria and I creaked as Logan plunked into it. Just dropped in.

Right in the middle of my date.

It was like he enjoyed taking his life into his own hands every time we interacted. I sucked in a sharp breath to try to rein in my irritation so I didn't scare my date off in the next five seconds.

"Any reason you're stopping by?" I asked him, making the mistake of glancing in his direction. His blond hair was styled in a way that showcased his sharp jawline and his defined cheekbones, and the infernal grin on his lips just taunted me. The light blue button-down he wore accented his dark eyes, and he had the sleeves rolled up, showcasing those tan arms.

"I saw you'd brought a new friend to Jake's, and I couldn't resist coming to say hi," Logan said, batting his lashes in my direction. He then pivoted to face Daria, extending a hand. Not like he'd attempt to steal this date, since he didn't swing her way, but Logan couldn't turn down an opportunity to cockblock me. "Great to meet you. Is this guy giving you a grand tour of our delightful Collier's Creek?"

My jaw clenched so hard I thought I heard it pop.

Daria simply grinned. "Well, we're starting with dinner and seeing where the night goes."

I appreciated that she gave him the clear direction, but Logan didn't budge.

"And you took her to Jake's?" Logan said, thwacking me on the arm. My fingers tightened into a fist. "Come on, we've got flashier bars than this one."

"Except you're clearly here instead of those ones, so I'm guessing this is where all the locals go," Daria said, engaging him further. We'd just met, so I couldn't just pass her a few timely eye signals to tamp down on the extra conversation. Give Logan a word and he'd yammer on for five minutes—or five hours.

"You'd be right," Logan continued. "I work at the bookstore up the road with Coop here. Have you been yet?"

Daria shook her head, not seeming irritated in the slightest. I wasn't sure if that was a good thing or not. On the positive, her cavalier attitude meant she seemed to be able to roll with the punches, but on the flipside, she hadn't given Logan an impetus to get the fuck out. My chest was burning, which happened so often around him that I wondered if I should take a Pepcid to prevent getting an ulcer.

"Your profile said leatherworker, not bookstore," Daria said. "Career switch?"

"Nah," I responded, leaping on the chance to try to steer the conversation back to reasonable. "It's my grandfather's shop, and he broke his leg recently, so I'm helping out for the time being."

"Please tell me you're a reader," Logan said, turning to Daria again. The slightest hint of a grin graced his lips, because clearly the bastard was enjoying divebombing my date. My insides heated up, and my palm twitched, the irrational urge to spank him rising within me.

"I like all types of fantasy, though my favorite is *A Song of Ice and Fire*," she said. I tried to restrain my groan, but it slipped out anyway. Before I could say anything, Logan dove in.

"A *Game of Thrones* fan? I've got some *opinions* on the books and even more on the series," Logan started, his zeal reaching his eyes. I noticed how the total enthusiasm morphed his features at the bookshop whenever he spoke about all the stories he loved with the customers.

While I was a casual reader, the bookstore was clearly his element, which was probably why he'd become such an asset to Gramps there.

"I was so angry about how the series ended," Daria leapt in, and I tilted my head back and stared at the wood paneling of the ceiling. Getting this date back on track would take hours now. Logan had the sort of energy and spark that seemed to draw everyone in, and he could engage people effortlessly—everyone except me. Because from high school on, he'd decided to be relentlessly annoying until the mere sight of him made my pulse pick up.

"What party's going on here?" The second I recognized this voice, I knew my date was officially over.

Logan wandering over had been bad enough, but now my family had descended.

"Come join us." Logan waved over to my younger brother Jordan, pointing to the empty seat. As if this was his hangout in the first place and he hadn't just crashed my date.

"Bro, did you hear Sadie named her gopher after me?" Jordan said, plunking into the seat. His thick hair was mussed, and he was still wearing his mechanic jumpsuit from work that reeked of motor oil. Jordan scanned over the three of us before a grin broke out on his face, a knowing in his eyes that made it clear he was aware what he'd disrupted as well.

"Yes, because her gopher's a moron and she saw the likeness," I muttered, beginning to rub at my temples. This was the last place I should've come to with a date. I knew better, and yet I'd wanted to be comfortable tonight, not surrounded by a bunch of strangers and loud music.

"Why wasn't I invited to this?" Kai said, announcing himself upon approach. I contemplated slamming my forehead on the table a bunch of times for good measure but decided against it.

Kai's wife Shelby strolled up behind him. She was short and compact, her long dark brown hair swept into a ponytail. The pretty peach A-line dress she wore highlighted her curves perfectly.

"Pull over a chair," I muttered. At least if Kai and Shelby were here, I could divert my attention to them rather than the menace who'd dropped in and destroyed my date before it had even begun.

Not like sparks flared between me and Daria or anything, which was a damn shame because she was beautiful and chill as hell.

Logan's leg jostled against mine from beneath the table as he moved his chair over to make space for Kai. The simple brush of our legs had my body flaring to awareness, which was the exact thing I'd been trying to escape tonight. He passed me a quick glance, those doe eyes briefly innocent, thick lashes framing them. But just as fast, the wicked amusement returned to them, and he launched back into the conversation with Daria.

"Do you think you could take my babysitting shift for Jordan Jr.?" my brother Jordan asked.

My brow wrinkled, but before I could respond, Kai leapt in. "Who's this? Do you have some child you accidentally fathered out there?"

"It's my sister's new gopher," I stepped in, before this spiraled any further out of control.

It would be one long-as-hell night.

Three beers later, and the annoyance had somewhat faded.

My libido, on the other hand, was dissatisfied as fuck.

Not only had I hoped to be getting laid tonight, but the very guy who had been bringing it roaring to life all week had insisted on sitting next to me the entire time. Logan's constant jostles and brushes had driven me insane, and I was ready to toss him out a window. Kai and Shelby had ditched about an hour after they showed up, and Jordan followed soon after. Logan finished the second beer he'd taken ages nursing and finally decided to leave.

"See you tomorrow," he said, blowing me a kiss.

"Hmm," I grunted out, not sure what to do with that one or with the way my gaze lingered. Most of the time, he acted condescending or downright irritating. If it were anyone else on the planet, I'd say he might even be getting flirty with me, but Logan had made it clear all the way back in high school what he thought of me. All the years in between, he'd just spent time cementing my view.

My gaze switched back to my date, who I'd barely managed a conversation with beyond my original one. Jordan and Logan had kept her engaged for most of the night, not letting me get a word in edgewise.

"Sorry about all that," I said, scratching my nape. I took a final sip from my lukewarm lager before placing the glass on the counter with a thump.

Daria barked out a laugh. "No apologies necessary. This was such a fun night." She paused and gave me a look. "Though, clearly not a date."

Heat rushed to my cheeks. Yeah, I'd fucked that up big-time once I decided to take her to Jake's Tap. "Would apologizing again mean anything?"

She snorted. "Don't worry about it. I had an absolute blast. Even if your ex-boyfriend was obvious as anything."

My brow crinkled. "Ex-boyfriend?"

Her eyes widened. "Oh, so he's just massively into you."

"Who?" I asked, feeling a bit like an idiot with the way she stared at me.

"Logan," she said as she began to rise from her seat. "That boy is so smitten with you it's ridiculous. It's been great, Cooper. Maybe we can hang out next time I'm in town."

Daria sauntered toward the door. I didn't realize my jaw was still dropped until she disappeared out the exit.

My thumb rubbed against the empty glass as I clutched it, staring at the door.

That was ridiculous. Logan had spent the past ten years annoying me.

Smitten?

No fucking way.

Chapter Eight

Logan

I toted Gramps's "contraband" in the two grocery bags on either side as I strode up the walkway toward his house. The place reminded me of home more than my childhood one did—or at least what I'd always imagined home would be like. It was a small rancher with white paneled siding, a tan roof, and a few flowering azalea bushes out front. The walkway remained in decent repair, and the welcome mat featured a stack of books, which fit him.

Once upon a time, there'd been a Gran Ellis in the household too, but she'd passed a few years ago, right before I started working at Ellis Books. Gramps had been hurting, and so was I, and we'd spent a lot of long hours bonding as he recounted stories of his late wife while I added the occasional diatribe about my mother. Our relationship hadn't always been glowing, but she'd stuck around when my father hadn't, so I gave her credit where it was due.

Upon reaching the door, I didn't bother knocking. He'd grumbled enough whenever I did it that I just stopped. The place had the same old-books scent as Ellis Books, though this was also threaded with orange, probably from the peels Gramps kept saving for his backyard garden. Or witchcraft? More likely witchcraft. The radio could be heard even from here, the entrance leading straight to the living room on one side and the bedrooms to the left. He'd probably be in the kitchen.

I swung the bags from side to side as I approached. "Hey, Gramps. I've got your crack."

When I stepped inside, I crossed my arms. Gramps stood at the stove cooking, the radio blaring, and his crutches nowhere in sight. "Okay, where are they?"

He glanced back. "By the sofa. I was fine getting over here without them."

I sucked in a breath. A good chunk of his family, Coop included, were all as stubborn as him. I utilized a different tactic than their typical badgering. "You forget I can withhold what's in these." I lifted my grocery bags.

Gramps heaved a sigh. "Fine, I'll go get them."

"Even better, I will," I said, heading into the other room before he could attempt to hobble over. The crutches were lying haphazardly on the side of the couch, like he said. As I grabbed them, another wave of sadness washed over me. If I wasn't working at Ellis Books, would I still be welcome over here? In the past few years, Gramps had become closer to me than the aunt I lived with.

When I stepped back into the kitchen, I noticed the trail of steam from whatever cooked in the stockpot he was tending to. I sidled up to him and set the crutches to lean against the wooden countertops. "Who are you cooking for, Gramps?"

"Have you seen the amount of people who tromp through here on a daily basis? If I don't have something prepared, we'll all starve," he said, his lips curling with a hint of a grin.

"Better question, what are you making, and is it almost done?" I asked, setting the grocery bags down on the counter with a crinkle.

"And here are your Swedish Fish. Make sure to hide them before Mary or Len show up and toss your contraband in the trash can."

"My teeth are fine," he muttered. "Just lost a few in the process."

I snorted. Far be it from me to deny the man the small joys of life, even if Swedish Fish ranked pretty low on my candy list.

"I'm making elk stew," he said, giving it another stir. "Jared swung by with extra elk from his hunting trip last week, so I might as well do something with all this time on my hands. What's happening at the shop? Has it caught on fire? Did someone steal my copy of *A Tale of Two Cities*?"

"Look, that book is not worth the fortune you think it is," I said, taking another whiff. The savory scents of elk and vegetables cooking together in broth was enough to make my stomach rumble. "You'd be lucky if people realized what book they were even stealing at this point. Besides—" I gave him a pointed stare "—with the gossip mill around this town, you'd know if anything happened to your shop before I even got in contact with you."

Gramps wrinkled his brow. "I hate being away from it for so long." A slight shadow slipped over his gaze as he glanced around the kitchen. This place was filled with memories for him, and while there were plenty of good ones of his wife, he'd made a concerted effort to spend plenty of time outside of the home ever since she passed. I didn't have the same nostalgia for the home I'd grown up in with my mom—just a shit double-wide on the fringes of town—but I got what he was going through.

"You'll be back soon," I said, clapping a hand on his shoulder. "But if you need a jailbreak, you've got my number. We can even go for a ride and yell obscenities out the window."

Gramps's eyes crinkled around the edges. "You could teach my family a thing or two about lightening up."

My heart squeezed tight and my grin widened, even as the guilt all but dripped through me at this point. The idea of leaving made me feel sick. I loved working at the bookstore, and Gramps had turned the place into such a home for me.

The creak of the front door snagged my attention.

"Another one of your visitors?" I asked, arching an eyebrow.

"I told you I was making food for a reason," Gramps said, a twinkle to his eye I didn't trust. The heavy footsteps should've been tipoff enough, but a second later, the mischief in his gaze made sense.

Coop stepped into the kitchen. His dark hair was windswept, and his stained sleeves were rolled to his elbows, a few streaks of god knew what up his arms. Chances were, though, he just smelled like leather, which made me think of sex. Probably inappropriate thoughts for his grandpa's house, but hey, my cock had gotten hard at an interview, so it clearly knew no bounds.

The moment we locked eyes, his expression darkened.

Not the exact response I wanted to inspire in him, but fair since I'd cockblocked his date last night. In my defense, I'd been horny and bored, which was a dangerous combination.

"Didn't realize Logan would be here," he said to Gramps, pointedly ignoring me.

Gramps still had a smirk on his face—because he'd done this intentionally. Somehow, he'd figured out my crush on his grandson years ago, and he'd made it clear he approved. Not like Coop would ever be interested though. I'd just delight in tormenting him until he ended up married to some Barbie or Ken of his dreams.

"I know you missed me," I said, deciding to dive right in. "But god, Coop, it was just last night. You can handle less than twenty-four hours without me."

Coop grunted, which I recognized as his way to not launch into snipes in front of others. Couldn't have everyone else seeing him as less than perfect.

"I'm glad both of you are here," Gramps said. "I've got a lot of stew, and I wanted to catch you up on what the doc said about my leg."

I placed a hand on my hip. "Couldn't have told me that earlier?"

Gramps grabbed bowls from his cupboards and began to ladle stew into them. When he plunked spoons in, I hustled forward to snag them from him, because the stubborn old man looked ready to try to hike over to the kitchen table with them, ignoring his broken leg.

"Thanks, Gramps," I said, balancing all three as I moved fast over to the table. Once I set them down in the spots with the clink of the spoons to the bowls, I plunked into a seat. Coop was hovering around Gramps, as if he would carry him over or some shit. I'd like to see him try. Gramps would hit him with a crutch.

I blew on the surface of the stew, full of chunks of meat, rich gravy, carrots, potatoes, and whatever spices Gramps had thrown in. It smelled delicious. Gramps was moving at a slow pace on purpose now, mostly because Coop wouldn't give him space. I watched the two go back and forth, Coop's jaw working with his frustration and Gramps's eyes glinting in amusement. We both enjoyed annoying Coop in our own ways.

Gramps settled across from me at the table, forcing Coop to sit between us on the end. I shook my head, biting on the inside of my cheek to restrain my grin. Old man never ceased to crack me up.

"So, explain the news from the doctor," Coop said, driving straight to the point. "Why didn't you contact Dad about this?" He sat in front of the stew like it wasn't even tempting him, but god only knew the man always had more discipline than I did. I scooped up some meat and veggies and ate a scorching mouthful. The burst of salt and heat on my tongue was worth the slight burn.

"Your parents already know the latest from my doctor," Gramps said, waving him away. "Doctor Crane said I'd be able to ditch the crutches by next week. Since that means I can sit behind the desk at the bookstore, I'll be able to get back to work—at least on the days you're currently covering, Coop."

Disappointment fluttered through me. As much as I hadn't expected anything to change between Coop and I in the time we worked together, spending so much time with him had sent a secret thrill through me.

"Did Doctor Crane give you the okay to return to work, or is this you going stir-crazy?" Coop said, picking up the spoon to jab it in his grandfather's direction.

"As long as you leave the restocking to me, we've got a deal," I said, extending a hand across the table.

Gramps broke out into a broad smile and shook. "I knew I could count on you."

"No, no, no," Coop interrupted. "You can't have possibly run this by your doctor or Mom and Dad. The risk of making your injury worse is too high." Then Coop swung his pendulum gaze my way. "And stop encouraging him."

"You should understand by now I do what I want," I teased back.

Coop's brows drew together, a scowl blooming on his face. Hot, hot, hot. "I'm well aware of that."

"As much as I appreciate the concern, my boy, I'll be returning to work as soon as I'm able," Gramps said, already half finished his stew, as if he'd inhaled it. "I just wanted to let you both know so you could make arrangements as need be."

Coop let out a grunt and tucked into his stew. I continued to spoon it into my face, mostly to avoid getting between the standoff between Stubborn and Stubborner.

Gramps set his spoon into his bowl with a clink. "I'm going to head over to my recliner to get my feet up. The long hour of cooking is starting to make my leg throb."

Coop's jaw tightened, but he held back his comment—probably about how Gramps needed more rest.

"I'll take your bowl over and clean up," I said. "Least of all I could do for the meal."

"Thank you," Gramps said, a twinkle returning to his gaze. I shook my head, amusement bubbling inside my chest. He was my hero. I wanted to be like Gramps Ellis when I grew up. Coop had risen and snagged the crutches to hand them over to Gramps who hobbled his way in the direction of the living room—leaving Coop and I by our lonesome.

The silence crackled between us, begging me to open my mouth and say something. Probably something to piss him off further, but that was what I seemed best at.

"You don't have to encourage him, you know," Coop said, his voice gruff. "He needs to be resting and recovering, not straining himself at the bookstore."

I fixed Coop with a look. His stubbornness clearly came from concern, and the snarky response melted on my lips. "I can manage him, Coop," I said, keeping my voice low. "He's not going stir-crazy in the house because he's bored."

Coop's brows drew together. Lord was this man dense. The clink of our spoons hitting the ceramic bowls echoed through the quiet as we continued to eat our stew.

"Memories of her are all around here," I murmured, my throat tightening with a weird mixture of grief and want that sometimes seized me. Loss for what I had and what I'd never experienced.

Coop stared at me in a way I'd never seen from him before, the intensity in those blue eyes making me shift in my seat.

"Fuck, why didn't I even think of that?" Coop muttered, swinging his gaze back to his bowl.

I chewed on my lower lip. For some reason, the flippant answers I usually gave him weren't emerging. "It's a grief thing."

Now I averted my gaze, just in time to catch Coop staring my way again. His eyes bored into me, but I felt stripped down. This wasn't what we did. We sniped at each other, and I annoyed him, which kept him at a comfortable distance.

"You lost your mom a few years back, right?" Coop asked, his tone foreign as well, not the sharp one I was used to from him but softened around the edges. Fuck, I didn't want his sympathy. My skin prickled from it, and I swallowed hard.

"Don't try to nudge in on Gramps's and my Grief Group," I said, trying to school my features to nonchalance. Unfortunately, I made the mistake of glancing up. Coop's mouth pressed in a firm line, but the intense way he watched me was unlike his normal reactions. Glib responses kept people at bay, kept them from the pitying looks that made me feel like shit. I had what I had, and I'd made do with it—hell, I'd carved out a pretty solid existence for myself.

Coop wasn't giving me pity doe eyes—I didn't think he was capable of it—but him taking me seriously was almost as bad. Because I'd wanted him to notice me for so long, but not just as a sympathy case.

"I'm serious. We trademarked the term and everything," I said, jabbing a finger in his direction, needing to drive this train past Sentimental Station.

Coop lifted his hands. "You can keep your trademarked Grief Group," he said before pinning me with his gaze again. "Thanks for the insight though."

I swallowed the lump in my throat. My crush on Coop had always been annoying as hell, but this was worse. Because him being nice to me deepened the attraction, which I needed to move on from posthaste.

Ever since high school, I'd known that Coop would never be the one for me—after I'd pissed him off by "stealing his girlfriend". Despite my attempts to shut my crush down, my body and mind continued to gravitate toward him every time we ran into each other, which continued to be a problem.

But I couldn't keep circling around him like this. Not if I wanted to find a guy beyond a single night.

In a week, Coop would be returning to his normal life, and I needed to move forward with mine.

Chapter Nine

Cooper

F ox's Restaurant was bustling at this time of night.

Sadie and Jordan had wanted to meet up for dinner, and while I was suspicious, I couldn't help but drag myself out. Chances were, they would try to recruit me into some get-rich-quick scheme, like the time they thought buying a bunch of bees and a hive would enable them to have some massive honey operation. It ended up with a bunch of bees that got loose instead. A "sting" operation.

I ran my fingers through my hair as I approached the front door, my mind whirring. The last time I'd been here had been with Logan to discuss work at Ellis Books, and already, the brief reprieve from my personal business problems would come to an end. Next week would be my return to normal, and my chest was knotted in ropes about the shift.

To make it worse, I'd been noticing Logan more and more.

My body's attraction to him could no longer be ignored, no matter how much I tried to rationalize that he was the most aggravating human being on earth.

The door swung open before I could grab it myself, and Geraldine bustled by, ignoring that I stood in front of her. Her hair had a bluish-green tinge to the white curls today, like she'd dunked it in a vat of chlorine, and she seemed to be on a mission, not even pausing to acknowledge me. I caught the door before it closed and slipped inside. The rich scents of meat and cheese wafted my way—the specialty here at Fox's Restaurant for their evening fare, along with whatever weekly specials Mae decided on.

The seats were mostly filled, but I spotted Jordan and Sadie in a second. They huddled in the corner booth, and I was pretty sure I saw a cage next to Sadie. If she brought her pet gopher, I would throttle her. Mae was way too sweet and wouldn't put up a fuss, but guaranteed someone would complain, and it'd just result in a headache for everyone.

I hooked my finger into the pocket of my jeans as I stepped in front of my siblings, who were furtively discussing something, all leaned in and speaking low. Clearly, not to be trusted.

"Sadie, is that Jordan?" I asked, crossing my arms as I came to a halt.

Jordan's grin widened. He looked just like Mom, with her dark curls, except while Mom and I were more similar personality-wise, he was a bucket of chaos. "I'm right here. Don't you recognize your own brother?"

I heaved a sigh. Maybe I should've ignored their texts. Granted, then my siblings would've shown up on my doorstep.

"He was lonely," Sadie said, sticking out her lower lip in an attempt at a pout. Not like my sister could pull it off—she didn't look remotely contrite.

"He's a fucking gopher," I said, taking a seat next to Jordan in the booth. The worn vinyl crinkled as I settled in. "He'd be fine if you popped him outside and let him run free."

Sadie glared at me. "Don't you dare. Jordan Jr. is injured and needs all the care he can get."

"What inspired the name?" I asked, arching an eyebrow. Sadie wouldn't have picked that on her own if she wasn't getting something out of it.

She rested a hand on the cage. "Jordan was with me when I found him, and he said he'd help take care of him if I named the gopher after him."

"So, then what do you need me for?" I asked, wary about what this conversation entailed. Guaranteed, they'd be trying to ask a favor. If it were Daisy or Henry, I wouldn't suspect that—the two of them were self-sufficient and just called to bitch. However, Sadie and Jordan had been getting themselves into trouble since we were kids. Both of them had always managed to be functional when it counted—holding down jobs, apartments, but I swore they caused trouble just to annoy me.

"You've got a lot of ranch contacts, yeah?" Jordan asked.

I stared at the ceiling, swallowing my groan. Fiona, the waitress swung by and made eye contact with me. All it took was a nod, and she bustled off to get my usual. Mae's wife had been working alongside her since they opened, and I'd never met anyone with a better memory. Granted, my coffee and burger order wasn't a hard one to remember, and I rarely deviated.

"Are you trying to find land where you can release this gopher?" I asked. "Because I'm telling you, take him out back and open the cage. Problem solved." Little squeaking sounds were coming from under the blanket covering the cage, tossed there as if Sadie could flimsily hide the fact she smuggled a wild animal into the restaurant.

"No, so we were thinking of trying to rent a plot of land," Jordan jumped in, his eyes flashing. "A small animal farm would be a lot of fun, and it would give Jordan Jr. and others like him a place to stay."

"Oh, and what's going to fund this small animal farm?" I asked, crossing my arms again. I had the feeling I might as well keep them that way for the rest of the night.

"Well, we'll obviously have some goats, so we can offer goat's milk," Sadie said, stroking the blanket overtop the cage as if she were petting Jordan Jr. by proxy.

"So, your entire venture will be funded by goat milk," I responded, my head starting to throb. My leatherworking business was at least a legitimate one, and even that was tough to keep afloat. The idea of my siblings popping off on a lark to take care of a bunch of animals fueled on farmer's market hopes and dreams made me want to slam my head through the wall.

"And a petting zoo," Jordan pitched in.

"A wild animal petting zoo." Well, that had liability stamped all over it. Chances were, this passing thrill would get tossed into their heaping pile of ideas once the two of them realized what hard work taking care of animals was, let alone wild ones. In the meantime, my big-brother job was to prevent them from investing too much into it.

"Yeah, like Jordan Jr. and some skunks, rabbits, maybe a pika," Sadie said, dead serious, because she believed this wouldn't be a wild animal blood-fest in a matter of a day.

"And you want me to contact the ranches I work with to see if they have space for your carnival of horrors?" I asked.

"Here's your coffee, Coop," Fiona said, placing the steaming cup in front of me.

"Thank you so much," I said, wrapping my hands around the porcelain as if the warmth from it would replicate the sanity I was losing from this conversation. Sadie frowned at me at this point, mostly because she'd figured out I wasn't going to contact the ranches in her stead. Jordan leaned back. He never went full-bore into these schemes. Usually he'd get distracted by the next shiny idea to travel his way.

"Why do you have it out for Jordan Jr.?" Sadie asked, flicking the paper from her straw wrapper across the table at me.

"Sadie, you picked this gopher up a few days ago," I said, maintaining a calm voice despite the rising urge to find the nearest empty table and enjoy a quieter dinner. "Where's the need to uproot your life to devote yourself to small critters coming from?"

"Blame Disney," Jordan said, cracking a grin. "Setting unreasonable forest critter expectations."

My forehead wrinkled as I caught the whiff of something foul that was definitely not the normal smells of Fox's Restaurant. Sadie's nose twitched, and my gaze landed on the crate.

"Did your gopher just shit in his cage?" I asked.

Sadie glanced off to the side, not making a move to peel back the wool blanket on her peeping disaster known as Jordan Jr.

"You can't leave the shit in his cage," I hissed. "We're in a restaurant, Sadie. It was bad enough you brought him in here in the first place, but you can't have the stench spreading through the place."

Sadie moved the blanket off the cage and her nose wrinkled. "Oh, gross."

"You'll be in for heaps of that with your wild animal petting zoo," I muttered.

"At least he kept the mess to the blanket he was napping on," Sadie said, going to hide the cage again.

I blinked. Lord, were my siblings in their twenties or still in grade school? "Give me the shit blanket, Sadie. I'm throwing that in the dumpsters out back."

She shrugged. "If you want it so badly, sure." She reached in and nudged Jordan Jr. before wrapping the shit into a neat parcel with the edges of the blanket.

I snagged it by the clean edges and pushed up out of the seat. "I'll be right back. Please keep Jordan Jr. from setting the restaurant on fire." With that, I made my way to the front door, trying to garner as little notice as possible. The stench wafting from the parcel was noxious, and I swallowed a gag. We were making this dinner as short as possible to avoid any more shit incidents from Sadie's goddamn gopher.

The brisk air was so welcome as I stepped out into the night, a yellowish light beaming down out front. I sucked in a crisp lungful, trying to dispel the horrible smell of Jordan Jr.'s shit. Shadows settled over me as I looped around the side of the building, making a beeline for the dumpsters in the back. I pushed the black lid up and slung Jordan's likely contaminated shit into the bowels of dumpster hell. I would need to scrub my hands.

My shoulders relaxed as I strolled back toward the restaurant. Before I swung around to the front of the building, voices drifted my way.

"He's leaving the shop next week—"

I recognized the voice at once. Logan. I stopped and leaned against the side of the building. If I wasn't misunderstanding, he was clearly talking about me.

"Wait, isn't that a good thing though?" a female voice responded—Penny, of course. Even after the brief stint the two of them had dated in high school, they remained best friends.

A huff sounded, definitely Logan, and the footsteps stopped. "Yes? No? Look, I know I've dodged around it for years, but you have to realize by now that I've had a crush on him forever."

My eyes widened, and shock rushed through my system.

"Shit, really?" Penny said. "Logan, I thought the comments around town were just jokes."

I sagged against the brick siding, my mind whirring faster than I could keep up with.

"I love you, sweetheart, but you are so bad at reading people," Logan responded. "Yeah, ever since high school."

"Even when I asked you to be my beard to get out of the relationship with him?"

My hand balled into a fist on instinct. Of fucking course. Considering Penny was a lesbian, and Logan was gay, I should've pieced that together sooner. Embarrassment flushed through me in a fierce sweep that I'd missed so much of the obvious in my tunnel vision. It'd been easier to be pissed at Logan for stealing my girlfriend, and then he'd made a pastime of antagonizing me.

"Logan," Penny continued. "You should've told me! I would've never asked you to pretend we were dating if I knew you liked him."

"It was a stupid crush, Pen," Logan muttered. "Not like anything would've ever come from it anyway. Come on. Let's go and get some food, so I can pretend this conversation never happened."

The door let out a creak and then a subsequent thump as they must've entered the building. My heart pounded harder as his words filtered through me. Logan Nichols liked me. I took a few steps forward, only spotting the yellowed light cast over the entryway, not him.

All the attraction wasn't one-sided, and more than that—had he been tormenting me for years on purpose?

The answer sat heavy in my chest with the weight of the realization.

Well, goddamn.

Chapter Ten

Logan

I closed my laptop, ready to be finished for the day. Tomorrow I had a second interview for the stupid job that had been hanging over my head like a perpetual raincloud, and I planned on grabbing takeout and then curling up with a book before crashing out early.

Ellis Books was quiet at this time of the day, mere minutes from closing. A lazy afternoon vibe spread through the place, along with the dust motes floating through the air. It was a contradiction to this morning when we'd been bustling with a bunch of newcomers who were in for a skiing weekend.

A shadow darkened the framed glass door at the entrance, and I heaved a sigh. Apparently I'd have to help one more person before I could escape for the evening.

The door creaked open, and Coop stepped inside. My brow crinkled.

"Did you leave something here on your shift yesterday?" I asked, peering at the sides of the desk, as if I might spot more than stacked books.

"Anyone still around?" he asked, his voice thick and gruff.

"Nah, I was just about to close," I said, pushing up from my seat behind the desk.

Coop reached behind him for the deadbolt, and the click of the lock echoed through the entire shop. "Good."

I took a few paces forward but hesitated. What the hell was Coop doing here? He began a slow approach my way, those powerful thighs flexing, his muscled arms swinging by his sides. Fuck, he was walking porn. Before I realized it, Coop wasn't stopping, continuing until he stood mere inches from me. I took a step back on instinct, trying to give him space. Coop followed with another step forward.

Intensity crackled between us, those blue eyes of his ablaze.

I backed up another few inches until I bumped against the shelves. My heart sped as he prowled forward with the graceful intent of a predator. Coop halted, and he brought his hand to the shelf beside me, crowding me against it. My mouth went dry.

This close, I couldn't help but notice everything—those thick brows, the serious purse of his lips, the way his dark hair swept down, long enough to tug on. His leather smell surrounded me, and my cock had already begun to stiffen from all the aggression pouring off him.

"You want my attention?" he asked, his low voice husky. A shiver rolled through me, and words evacuated my brain.

I opened my mouth, but all I managed to do was lick my lips. Coop's eyes followed the motion, and his nostrils flared.

"All the pranks, the annoyances, the taunts," Coop continued. "That's because you wanted my eyes on you, right, Lo?"

Oh holy fuck.

Was this a dream? Definitely a wet one. My cock throbbed, my erection straining against my jeans, and I was about to combust.

"My eyes are on you now," Coop rasped out. His arm still braced along my side, he leaned in and closed the space between us.

I'd imagined Cooper Ellis's lips on mine a million times over the past decade.

Nothing compared to the reality.

His mouth was rough and hot, the sensations making me melt in an instant. Cooper wasn't the sort of man who kissed—no, he possessed, and I'd been wanting for far too long to be claimed by him.

The ridges of the books pressed against my back as I sank against the shelf behind me, letting him take the reins. My entire body felt alive, like sparks raced through each limb, down to each finger and toe, the pleasure a shock to my system. His other hand wrapped around my nape as he kissed me deeper, the calluses from his palm scratching against my skin. A moan slipped from my lips before he swallowed it down with another kiss.

My mind spun, unable to catch up to the fact that Cooper Ellis was kissing me right now. So, instead of questioning it, I gripped onto the fabric of his shirt and held on for the ride.

His tongue swept into my mouth, and my lashes fluttered as I savored the way he consumed me, how his kisses grew deeper, more intense with every pass. I could live in this moment forever, pinned in place by this man, surrounded by his intense heat, with his mouth on mine. Even the slight discomfort of the books pressing against my back barely registered compared to the euphoria that buzzed through me, waking up parts of myself I'd long forgotten existed.

The chemistry between us was nothing short of legendary, but somehow I'd always suspected it would be. I'd never experienced the draw to another man like I did to Cooper Ellis, and this kiss confirmed it.

He bit down on my lower lip, the sting sending a bolt of pleasure through me, before he licked over it to sooth it away. His grip was tight on my nape, like he held me in place, and my eyes rolled back at just how good that felt. This man emanated pure sex, all raw and masculine in a way that had me reeling, and a whimper escaped me. My cock ached at this point, and I was so turned on I could barely breathe, but there was no way in hell I'd stop kissing Coop.

When he pulled back, his shoulders were heaving, and his pupils were blown with lust. Seeing the reddened lips on him, the naked desire in his eyes had me so hot I couldn't focus on anything but him. Hell, part of me wanted to flip around and offer my ass, because god, I needed him any way I could get him while he was in the grips of whatever madness had inspired this.

"Fuck, that mouth. So goddamn sexy," Coop said, his lips curling into a smirk. My heart all about stopped. "Is this the way to get you to shut the hell up, beautiful?"

He was taunting me, for sure, but my brain pretty much stalled on the fact that Coop had just called me beautiful. My chest exploded into butterflies.

"Not sure." I finally pushed the words out. "Might need some more testing."

He shook his head, his eyes crinkling at the edges. God, this man was breathtaking. Coop slid his hand along my waist, placing his massive thigh between my legs, and I couldn't help but grind against him.

"Goddamn," he swore, his husky voice my undoing. "You want more?"

I licked my lips, my gaze drifting to his cock. "If you're offering," was all I managed to get out. I sank down to my knees, easy to do since they were already trembling, and then looked up at him. If I thought up close was hot, staring at Coop towering over me was even hotter. His hand drifted to his belt buckle, the jangling noise making my mouth water. His bulge was prominent as fuck in the front of his Wranglers, and I wanted to take every inch of it.

He unbuckled his belt, then unzipped his jeans, the sounds achingly loud in the loaded air. The whole time, Coop stared down at me, the tension in the air like the sky before a tornado. His eyes were near black with lust, and the heat in his expression coursed through my whole body, lighting me up. I'd never in a million years believed Coop would stare at me like that, and I couldn't pass up this chance.

"You look hot as hell on your knees, Nichols," he said, the huskiness of his tone pure sex. He nudged his boxer-briefs down and drew his cock out. "Like you could swallow me whole."

"Ngh," slipped out from me, because apparently my eternal wit failed me when faced with Cooper giving me sex eyes. Plus, god, his cock was beautiful. The perfect length to slam into my prostate and nice and thick, enough to make me feel full as hell. The flushed head glistened with pre-cum, and my mouth watered for a taste.

He wrapped his hand around the base of his cock and directed the tip to rest on my lower lip. My tongue dipped out to swipe at the slit, the burst of salt exploding on my tongue.

"Fuck," Coop swore, and his lashes fluttered. A sense of power rushed through me, a damn heady thing. I batted his arm away and settled in front of his cock. When Coop's fingers threaded through my hair instead, I didn't bother restraining my moan. I loved a little pain with my sex, and if he was as aggressive as I hoped, fuck, that was dangerous—because I'd always been low-key obsessed with this man.

I licked at his tip, enjoying running the end of my tongue around it in circles as I reached down and undid the button of my pants, unzipping next. Once I dragged my cock out, I gave it a few strokes, licking and lightly sucking on the tip of Coop's cock. My teasing must've been getting to him, because he tightened his grip on my hair enough that it stung, which made my mouth water more.

I gave him another light suck and looked up to flutter my lashes.

"Brat," he growled, tugging at my hair again. I moaned around his tip, unable to help myself. "Keep teasing, and I'll just shove it in."

Yes, please.

I met his gaze, daring him to follow through. Leaning forward, I gave one more deliberate kitten lick.

Coop's brows lifted until a wicked grin split his face. "You asked for it," he said, his grip tight on my hair as he thrust in. I gagged a little at the sudden intrusion, a little drool slipping from my lips. He lifted his brows, but I gave my head the slightest bob. I wanted him to fuck my face so badly.

The weight on my tongue, the velvet feel of him was sin, and my mouth was watering nonstop as he slid down my throat. I gagged again a little, and he backed off to give me a breath before driving right back in. This dominant side of Coop was everything I could've hoped for. I began to breathe through my nose as Coop found a rhythm, taking it slow even as he held my head in a vise grip with his fingers threaded through my hair. The man smelled like musk and leather, and his cock was so damn delicious.

My knees bit into the hardwood. Fuck, I was kneeling on the floor of Ellis Books with the glass door and broad windows out front while sucking Coop's cock. However, with the way the sting from his grip sent shocks of pleasure through me, I couldn't care less. He drove into my mouth again and again, using me like a fucktoy, which got me hotter. My balls ached at this point, my cock dripping.

My vision glazed over, and I blinked away tears as he continued to fuck my face, drool dripping from me like a faucet. His dark hair drifted across his forehead, and his brow creased with concentration as he levelled all his focus on me. I'd been chasing after it for years, and being the object of this man's attention was a heady thing. My mind reeled from how he consumed me, both body and soul.

"God, I'm going to come," Coop groaned out. His pace was relentless—my throat would burn after this—and I reached down to jack my own cock. A few strokes had my balls drawing up. I'd been close to the edge the moment this man kissed me, and the tension coiled tight through me, a snapped thread away from spilling.

"Who knew," Cooper said, his husky voice my undoing. "You mouth off to me any chance you get, but you take my cock like a good boy."

Oh fuuuck.

My balls emptied, and I came. My cum splashed out onto the hardwood, and my eyes rolled back in my head as pleasure rushed through me with the force of a flash flood.

Coop stiffened, tugging on my hair as his cum shot down my throat. The groan that came from him was the hottest thing I'd heard in my life. I sat there on my knees as his cock kicked out another pulse, and my mouth flooded with his release. He slowly began to pull out, and his shattered breaths gave away how hard he'd come. Some of his cum dribbled down my chin, and I reached up to wipe it away with my forearm.

My body felt wrung out from the orgasm, and my gaze drifted to the puddle of cum on the hardwood I'd need to scrub up. Heat flushed my cheeks at the realization that I'd just sucked Coop off in the middle of the bookstore, where anyone could walk by and peer inside. And with how nosy everyone was, I wouldn't be shocked if someone had been gawking in on the show.

I still couldn't bring myself to care—not when I'd finally experienced the whirlwind that was Cooper Ellis.

He ran his thumb along my jaw, tilting my head up to look at him. "I was going to ask if I could return the favor, but it looks like you already came." His brow arched as he inspected my mess on the floor, and if anything, my cheeks burned hotter.

I'd spent years antagonizing him to keep all of *this* at bay—the fact that this man had drawn me in from the second I met him. The amount I was attracted to him was damn embarrassing, and somehow, he'd found out.

Coop reached down and grabbed my hand, helping me rise. My knees pretty much creaked with the effort after digging into the hardwood.

"Hey," he said, his voice coming out a bit gruff. "Are you okay? I didn't cross any lines, did I?" The concern flaring to life in those blue eyes made my heart flutter.

I licked my lips, which were spit-slicked and tasting a little coppery from how swollen they were. "All good here," I said, my voice a bit hoarse.

Coop let go of my hand, which I hated because the skin-to-skin contact was giving me a high all on its own. He crossed his arms, fixing me with one of those grumpily serious looks that usually drove me to annoy him. "I'm not used to you being this quiet. Are you sure what we did was all right?"

A snort escaped me. "What part of me dropping to my knees spelled 'not gagging for this?'"

Coop scanned me over, the heat in his eyes incendiary—and new. I still wasn't used to this man viewing me this way, which made me shiver. I slipped past him and tucked my cock away as I headed over to the desk. I grabbed the spray and paper towels I kept by there and walked back over to my puddle of cum. In a few quick swipes, it was all cleaned up, and the quiet radiated through the room, as if waiting for one of us to break it.

I tossed out the wad of paper towel and zipped up my pants before buttoning up. When I glanced up, Coop had silently moved and stood right in front of me all looming and serious and seriously sexy.

"Well," I said, nervous energy rushing through me. Maybe this had all been a huge mistake. Maybe Coop's fit of insanity was receding, and he questioned every second of what we'd done. "I better finish counting out and get out of here. Shop's closed." As if that wasn't obvious.

Coop stared at me for a moment. "You've got to be kidding if you think I'm about to let you just run out of here, Nichols. I'll wait for you to finish up, and then you're getting in my truck, and we're having a conversation."

I swallowed hard.

So much for fit of insanity.

Chapter Eleven

Cooper

My brain was still trying to process what I'd just done. I leaned against one of the shelves, trying to piece together how my plan of coming here to talk had morphed into all but shoving him against the wall, kissing him until he turned to putty, and then coming down his throat.

Hell, I'd even swung by Delilah's Café to grab BLT sandwiches since I figured he'd be hungry after finishing his shift. The stroke of politeness seemed a bit off note after all the aforementioned shit. I speared my fingers through my hair. I'd planned on confronting him once and for all, but when I'd stepped in and seen Logan sitting at the desk, his blond strands drifting over his forehead, the pouty lower lip thrust out enticingly—fuck, I hadn't been able to stop.

My legs had carried me across the room and then our bodies did the rest.

Logan focused intensely on counting the money in the till, not doing the usual yammering like he did during just about any activity. Seeing him off-kilter like this solidified everything I'd overheard, and I didn't know what to do about the realization.

I should've figured the sparks flying between us weren't just irritation all these years, and with the amount I'd been fixating on him lately—fuck. That had hands down been the best blow job I'd ever gotten, and not just from the talented way he'd sucked me down. The wildfire chemistry between us had amped everything even further. The quiet between us simmered with the unspoken, but while Logan relished in the irritation his words brought, I relished in this.

Quiet, I could handle.

He'd been upending my world for years, so it was only fair that he got to squirm a little bit. His blond hair was tousled from the way I'd gripped it, those strands like silk in my palms. And the little moans he made around my cock, how his lashes fluttered, the blissed-out look on his face when he came—all of that had cemented into my memory. How I was supposed to move on from this after witnessing the way he melted in my arms was beyond me.

Because I'd been searching for chemistry like this for a long, long while. I'd just never expected to find it right underneath my nose.

"All finished," Logan announced, moving the money into the safe tucked behind the desk. "Let the abduction begin." He avoided eye contact, even as he rose from his spot.

A slow smile rolled onto my face. "All I said was a little conversation."

Logan finally looked up at me, his gaze pointed. "You said getting in your truck, so my guess is we're going to do some talking, and then you're going to find an isolated place to murder me and hide the body, like you've always wanted."

Before today, hell before the past hour, I might've agreed with him. The man knew how to get me keyed up faster than anyone else on the planet. But that was before the foundation to what I'd believed to be mutual loathing had gotten shaken to the core.

"Seems like you've got me all figured out," I responded with a wan grin. In the past, the comments from Logan would've irritated me, but a large part of my annoyance had been because I'd been anticipating him saying something cutting—pulling some prank to piss me off. Ever since Penny had dumped me for Logan, I'd been viewing him in a negative light, expecting the worst out of him, but what I'd overheard had been a revelation.

"Where's the trademark irritation?" Logan asked, his brows drawing together. "The clenched jaw that makes you look constipated? The growling, like you've spent so much time out in nature that you've gone feral?"

Damn, what a difference information made. All those comments of his—they hadn't been just to dig under my skin. No, they were Logan's way at keeping me at a distance, which he'd been successful at for years.

Except now I'd gotten a taste, and I sure as hell wasn't finished with Logan Nichols.

"Come on," I said, ignoring his jabs. "Let's go."

Logan wrinkled his nose, the motion kind of fucking adorable. Hell, when he wasn't mouthing off at me constantly or adding to my general rolodex of problems, the man was beyond cute—he was sexy as sin.

"I'm sending an SOS to Gramps as assurance," Logan said as he walked in front of me, leading the way to the door. "If I'm not heard from after tomorrow, he'll avenge me."

I snorted, my gaze fixed on the perfect peach of an ass on clear display with those tight pants of his. He could walk in front of me all he wanted. Even though I'd just come my brains out minutes earlier, my flagging cock was giving a valiant attempt at rising again at the thought of sinking deep inside him. His mouth had been goddamn sinful, so I could only imagine how his ass would feel.

Logan stepped outside and I followed, the keys jangling as I locked up behind me. All the shiny glass in the front of the store mocked me with how reckless I'd been. Just unzipping my pants and coming down Logan's throat during the day, in the shop, where anyone could've peeked in and caught us. This man had always made me lose my mind, but I hadn't realized in how many ways.

My black Tacoma was covered in a thin film of dirt from the road, since I'd been driving from one handyman job to the next today. I should be in my shop, working on leather orders, but those were as dry as ever. Logan looped around to the passenger's side and cracked the door open, hopping in. Clearly, he wasn't that concerned about getting murdered.

I settled into the driver's seat, and the tension between us fucking crackled as I turned on the ignition. The truck rumbled beneath me, and I pulled out of my spot, gliding onto the road. The destination I had in mind would be a good spot to sit and talk—without any interruptions or the ability to play the avoidance game. I hadn't realized how skilled Logan was at it until discovering he'd been hiding a decade-long crush.

The radio station played quietly, some old rock music, so I turned it up a bit to give Logan a reprieve. He remained quiet and simmering, which was so unusual after years of listening to him snipe and sass at me whenever we saw each other. The town passed by in a blink as I sped along the road, the music blaring from the speakers. I rolled the windows down, bringing the sunshine and crisp scents in.

I stole a quick glance at Logan and all but swallowed my tongue. He leaned against the side of my car, propped on his elbow, and his gaze was fixed on the road ahead. With his blond hair whipping around, those pretty lips pursed, and a rare serious expression on his face, he was utterly gorgeous. Fuck, I wanted to veer off the road just to kiss him again, but that wouldn't happen until we had time to chat—the way I'd planned before I lost my mind.

"We're well out of town now," Logan said, his voice breaking through the music and the roar of the wind. "I was joking about you dragging me out into the middle of nowhere for nefarious purposes, but I feel like I should be getting concerned."

"Look, I just want to talk somewhere quiet," I said, scanning the horizon for the turnoff I searched for. The spot was about fifteen minutes outside town, nowhere that distant, but around here, large stretches of nature quickly overtook the landscape. Already, Collier's Creek was swallowed up by the looming mountains and the rolling green that stretched out in every direction. Out here, I could calm my mind enough to get to the bottom of whatever was going on between the two of us.

Because it was clear there was something, and now that I was aware, I wouldn't let him keep pushing me off and avoiding this.

The sign for Clark Lake was a dingy little green and white thing, and I turned off onto the dirt and gravel path. It crunched under my tires as we headed for the lot folks parked at. The late-afternoon sun cast everything in a gilded hue, and even from here, I caught glimpses of the lake from between the fringe of trees.

"Ah, so a boating accident," Logan said, his smart mouth beginning to slip into place again. Getting him to speak directly would be the biggest challenge.

However, for once, I had the advantage with this guy, and I wasn't going to pass up the opportunity.

"Can you grab the bag in the backseat?" I asked as I pulled into park. Logan undid his seatbelt and flipped around, digging for the sandwiches I'd picked up. My mouth watered when I caught the glimpse of his ass in the air.

The paper of the bag crinkled when he got it, and he glanced over to me. A slow grin spread to his lips. "You know, remote location like this, we could do a lot better things than talk."

I arched an eyebrow. "I got off track earlier, but you're not getting out of this."

"Well, you certainly got off," Logan said, waggling his brows as he settled in the seat.

"Come on," I said, cracking the door open. "Let's walk over to the lake."

"Boating accident," he sang back, seemingly recovered. However, as he stepped up beside me, I didn't miss the furtive glances he snuck in my direction or how he chewed on his lower lip like he was worried. Now that I was paying attention the right way, I was shocked at how I'd never realized his attraction before. It was obvious.

"What's in the bag?" Logan asked as we strolled along the narrow path that carved through the trees to the lake. Already being out here in nature settled me a little more, the trill of birdsong echoing in the distance. Escaping to the wilderness and crafting with leather were the two things guaranteed to help clear my mind, which I sorely needed right now. The wind carried the slight hint of spice and old books, all Logan.

"Figured you might be hungry since you finished up your shift," I said, hooking my thumb into the pocket of my beaten Wranglers. The golden sun soaked through my skin, and, that effervescent warmth combined with the orgasm I'd had before coming here had me all but buoyant at this point, the stress melting away.

"Did you get bodysnatched?" Logan asked, squinting my way. "You haven't sniped or grumbled at me yet, and you're being nice to me? I must've entered an alternate dimension."

Guilt flushed through me. Logan wasn't innocent—he'd done everything in his power to needle at me over the years, but I'd been so blinded by my initial opinion of him that I hadn't bothered to see the clear signs.

"Am I the last person to realize?" I asked, the words jumping to my lips.

Logan lapsed into quiet again, his glance flickering my way and back ahead again. The sight of Clark Lake stretching out before us stole my attention for a moment. The sunlight glittered across the bright blue expanse, so vibrant it was like a mirror to the sky. Trees dotted around the lake and the rocky shoreline trailed off to the edges. The mountains framed it perfectly, deep-set crags that sliced into the landscape.

"Realize what?" Logan said weakly. He'd run out of ways to avoid me, yet he still tried. I wasn't giving him the option.

"I overheard you and Penny talking the other night at Fox's," I said, coming to a halt alongside him in front of the lake. The water lapped up to the rocks a short distance away, and the quiet thrum of the water gave me the peace of mind to just cut to the chase. "About me."

Logan's swallow was audible. "Well, maybe I was feeding Penny a bushel of lies."

I reached over and gripped his chin, tilting his face in my direction. "Bullshit."

His thick lashes fluttered, a surprising vulnerability in those dark brown eyes. I thought I knew Logan Nichols, but I'd apparently gotten everything wrong. What I'd do about that, I didn't have the slightest, but I needed to make him aware of what had shifted.

"Fine," he murmured. "There may have been a crush, but it didn't matter. I was persona non grata ever since I stole Penny from you."

"Explain that," I demanded, letting go of his chin.

Logan licked his lips, a motion which was fast hardwiring my brain for sex. "Not everyone was able to easily come out, Coop. Your family's always been accepting. Penny realized she was a lesbian and needed a beard. We've been best friends since we were little, so I didn't hesitate to masquerade with her until we finished out high school."

Guilt thrummed through me. He wasn't wrong. I'd met Penny's parents a few times, and while they were okay, they maintained some pretty rigid views.

"What about your family?" I asked, needing to know. Logan was aware of so much with me while I had a massive gap in my knowledge when it came to him.

"All I had was my mom," he said with a shrug. "And she didn't love my 'choices,' but she stuck around. I listened enough to tell how she felt though, so I waited until I headed for college to come out publicly. Not like I didn't get around still."

No siblings, just his mom, and he'd lost her too. Suddenly, the irritation I'd always had toward him intruding on our family made me feel downright ugly. I'd been given a wealth of support and love from my chaotic family, and no matter how much they drove me crazy, I couldn't imagine walking through the world without them. I couldn't fathom how Logan had survived all these years with his unflappable sense of self intact.

"No," he said, slicing through the air. "None of the Poor Orphan Annie eyes. This is why I don't tell people."

I sucked in a breath. "Less pity and more feeling like a dick for the amount of shit I've given you over the years."

Logan cast me a direct look. "You and I both know I earned the shit you gave me honestly."

A laugh exploded out of me, a burst of pure lightness. "If you were looking to get my attention, you managed to achieve it."

"Maybe not the attention I wanted," he admitted, casting a glance to the rocks beneath our feet. "But the little line you get between your brows and your growly voice are really hot."

I shook my head, my shoulders quaking with amusement. "Here, let's get the food out." With that, I sat on the sun-warmed rocks and spread my legs. Logan set the paper bag between us and lowered himself down as well. He rummaged through to pull out the BLTs and bags of chips I'd grabbed—nothing fancy, but I'd wanted to make an effort. The way his eyes softened at the sight made my heart quicken.

"You didn't have to do this," he murmured. The rawness in his expression formed a direct contrast from every guarded, cocky comment he'd flung my way over the years, and I found myself fascinated. How I'd read him so wrong was a fucking mystery to me. There was an air of skittishness to him right now, like coaxing a wild animal, and I had the feeling if I addressed this head-on, he'd just bolt.

"So did the whole town know about your crush?" I asked, grabbing my sandwich and taking a bite. "I mean they've teased me about it, but I thought everyone was just in on a joke."

"Oh absolutely," he said, settling into place with his own food. "You and Penny were the only two who hadn't figured it out. Penny because she's as dense as a dying star when it comes to attraction, and you because you were too busy getting your feathers ruffled every time I wandered your way."

I snorted, shaking my head. "Well, damn." I licked a bit of the mayo from the side of my mouth, and Logan's gaze zeroed in on the motion.

"So, that's all out in the open," Logan said, his dark gaze heating up. "Where does that leave us now?"

"Million-dollar question, isn't it?" I responded, leaning forward a bit. "I'll be honest, I haven't felt chemistry like that in years—if ever. I'm not sure what any of this is, but don't for a second think I'm letting it go without a try. If you're in, let's see where this takes us."

"You want to explore?" Logan's eyes flickered with the palest hope.

"Truth?" I said, brushing my thumb under his chin again. "I want to devour you whole."

Chapter Twelve

Logan

Three days had passed since "The Great Bookstore Incident," and I was horny beyond all belief. Coop hadn't ghosted on me—we'd started texting, which was weird as fuck, to put it mildly. However, we also hadn't been able to sync our schedules up. A leatherworking client had booked him last-minute, so he needed to fit them in amid his time at the bookstore and his handyman jobs around town. Meanwhile, I kept busy with wallowing in guilt after the second interview with the stupid company.

I wanted the job for the relief it'd offer, but at the same point, I hoped they'd turn me down.

Today was the weekend though, and I'd been invited to Jordan's twenty-fifth birthday party, which was family friendly during the day and guaranteed to be a shitshow by the evening. Without a doubt, Coop would be there, and the temptation to fling myself at him rode me hard.

Nerves prickled as I pulled up in front of Jordan's place, a house on the outskirts of town that he rented with two other guys. The cabin made the perfect bachelor pad, and it didn't seem like any of them planned on moving on any time soon. Already, a bunch of familiar cars were parked out front—recognizable since I'd been getting invites to Ellis functions for the past three years. My chest squeezed tight. Who knew if I'd still be invited if I ended up leaving to work this remote job.

My gaze landed on a familiar Tacoma, and my pulse quickened. Coop and I had agreed to explore, but what that meant had my mind whirling. Considering he'd been messaging me ever since, trying to get to know me—fuck, my heart sped up at the thought. I shouldn't have been surprised Cooper Ellis would approach this with the same seriousness he approached everything else. My wildly colorful array of dildos was getting a workout at home though.

I sucked in a breath to prepare myself and hopped out of my car. The sounds of the Ellis family drifted my way from inside the house, the open windows carrying the noise. I ran my fingers through my hair, which I'd taken the time to style before coming. Hell, I'd spent more time in the shower, trimming up, washing everything, just on the off chance Coop decided to spirit me away to fuck my brains out.

Before I could touch the handle, the door swung open. Sadie stood in the entryway.

"Come on in, Logan," she called, reaching out to grab my hand and drag me in. "You've got to meet Jordan Jr."

My brows drew together. Either Sadie and Jordan had some incestuous love child or one of the five billion tourists Jordan slept with had ended up giving him a surprise baby. Still, I followed where Sadie directed me, past the entryway which was covered in tacky hunting décor—hello, deer heads—and too much camo. Instead of heading to the left into the living room where most of the noise came from, she brought me into a room to the right, which was an attempt at an office. A fuckton of papers sat on a desk wedged in the corner. The dartboard and basketball hoop took up most of the place.

And in the opposite corner of the room was a cage with a rumpled purple blanket over it. Sadie sank to a crouch to tug the blanket off. "Ta-da, Jordan Jr."

I blinked, staring at a small rodent—a fucking pocket gopher. "What the hell are you doing with one of those?"

"I rescued him," Sadie said proudly. The little guy squeaked at me, rushing to the edge of the cage like he was saying hi. My insides melted at the sheer cuteness of his tiny dark eyes. I dropped down to offer a finger to sniff.

"He's so adorable," I said, glancing up to Sadie.

A sharp sting drew my gaze down, just in time to see the little fucker sinking his teeth into my skin.

"Ow," I yelped out, pulling my hand away. "Shit, he bit me."

"Jordan Jr., that wasn't nice," Sadie reprimanded.

"Maybe you shouldn't be putting your hands into cages with wild animals." That all-too-sexy tone came from behind me, dry and deprecating.

I whipped around to glare at Coop as I clutched my finger. "Look, it was in a cage. I thought the thing had been domesticated." The site of the bite was beginning to throb at this point. Shit, weren't wild animal bites super infectious? "Am I going to die from this?'

Coop's arms were crossed as he stared at me, those bright blue eyes holding an amusement I was still adjusting to. I'd gotten levelled with his irritated stares for years, but this—the looks he tossed my way now held a warmth to them that made me shiver. Today, he oozed pure sex with those dark locks drifting over his forehead, his muscles all bunched up with his posture, straining the Henley he wore, sleeves rolled to the elbows.

"You'll be fine," he said. "But you should wash the cut out in case you get an infection."

I brought my bitten finger up, looking at the blood welling at the tip. Fuck, fuck, fuck. It definitely stung. Was it tingling? "I'm too pretty to die from a gopher bite." I shot to my feet, ready to bolt to the bathroom.

Coop snorted and walked over. He placed a hand on my lower back, a possessive move that sent a tiny thrill through me—soon drowned out by my imminent death at the merciless teeth of a tiny monster. Most of the noise came from the living room, but Coop guided me down the hallway leading to the bedrooms and into the first open door.

The bathroom was a bit cramped, but Coop brought me over to the sink and popped the water on.

"Let's get this taken care of," he said, bringing my hand under the stream of water from the faucet. Red from the dripping blood flowed into the stream, turning the water pinkish, but with the warm water rushing over it, some of the sting ebbed away. With the pain muted, all I could focus on was Coop crowding in next to me, holding my hand to the sink and taking care of me.

I'd been so in lust with him for years, but this was the real reason I'd been fine with our distance. Because for all the shit I gave him about being Mr. Perfect for everyone else, the truth was that despite Coop's seriousness and grumpiness, he was one of the most caring people I'd ever met. I'd watched him step up for his family and friends time and time again, and having his care directed my way?

Fuck, I'd be falling so fast my head would hit the pavement.

He squirted some soap over the offending gopher bite, and it stung as he washed it out, but I let him handle it anyway. Not like I would pass up the chance to get all up in Coop's space like this. His gaze remained firmly fixed on my finger and the task at hand, but I now knew what it felt like to have his singular focus pinned my way. It was heady as hell.

"It barely grazed you," Coop said, his rough voice full of gravel. A shiver ran through me in response. "But those things are infectious as shit, so keep an eye on the bite anyway. I've already had to deal with Sadie and Jordan getting several from their idiotic choice in pets."

"They get this special treatment too?" I asked, licking my lips.

Coop met my gaze. "No."

Fuuuuck, this man was so goddamn hot. My cock was stiffening from the proximity and the fact I'd been imagining him bending me over and taking me every which way. He emanated pure competence, which was a bigger turn-on than I realized. Still, I needed to pump the brakes a little. Coop clearly wanted to go another round with me, based on the way he stared at me right now—like he wanted to devour me—but my heart was already taking detours off Casual Lane.

"I wish I could ditch this and drag you away," Coop murmured, his voice all husky and hot.

He wouldn't ditch though, not on his family, which was one of the things I admired about him the most. I'd lived the repercussions of men who bailed, so the guys who were committed, the ones who stayed earned my respect every time.

"What, you're not loving the calendar Jenga we're failing at?" I responded, trying to ignore the jackrabbit pace of my heart. The gopher bite was all but forgotten at this point, and I faced Coop, mere inches separating us. The urge to close the space between us and taste his lips again reared up in a big way, and he eyed me like his mind was on the same track.

"I'm going fucking crazy," he growled, gripping my chin to turn my face in his direction. The move sent such a dose of adrenaline through me that I was floating. This attention from Coop was everything

I'd dreamed of for years, and he didn't disappoint in the slightest. The man's intensity would be my undoing. It made me forget about everything—my current worries, the fact we were at his family's function—all that existed was the two of us, here in this space.

I licked my lips, suddenly dry with the urge to lean up and taste him.

"Coop, don't kill Logan," a voice called from outside the bathroom. Daisy had stepped into the doorway.

Coop dropped his hand from my chin and took a step back, sending ice water splashing over me. Of course he didn't want his family to know. Hell, we hadn't even figured out what we were, but the move put the brakes on the rampant lust that had been flowing through me.

"He's just manhandling me a little," I announced, refusing to let the interruption get me down. "Joke's on him because I like that shit."

Daisy let out a laugh, her eyes bright with amusement. The rest of his family had been on board with my sense of humor years ago. Coop was the only one who'd loathed me. And hell, ten years of rivalry had flipped on its head in the span of a week.

"He got accosted by Sadie's stupid gopher," Coop muttered, placing a hand on my back again as he guided me forward out of the bathroom. The intimate gesture sent sparks flaring through me. This man was a goddamn roller coaster. All the small touches, the way he crowded into my space, just fueled my attraction to him. I'd thought he would back away given his family, but that wasn't the case.

"Maybe we can accidentally let the thing loose in the woods," Daisy murmured. "My kids keep trying to go into the office to take a peek."

"I'm shocked Harrison doesn't have his own menagerie by now," Coop said, talking to his sister as we strolled down the hall, his hand still on my lower back. Normally, my mouth would be running a mile a minute, but the feel of the heavy hand pressed there struck me speechless. The heat, the weight, the possessive move—Cooper Ellis was a dangerous man.

"He sticks to stray domesticated animals, thank you very much," Daisy responded, not paying attention to how Coop guided me forward. Considering we'd kept our distance from each other during parties in the past, the fact we were in the same proximity was groundbreaking enough.

We reached the living room, and Daisy entered first. Coop nudged me through the door, and I already missed the heat of his hand on my back. The wall of noise rushed into me, simply from having the Ellis family gathered in the area. Jordan's roommates Hal and Chad were hanging out talking to Henry and Coop's dad, and Gramps and Sadie were in a fierce conversation with Daisy's youngest, Jessie. Harrison and Jordan sat on the couch by the far wall along with Coop's mom. The sight was nothing like what I'd grown up with, mostly hanging by myself and a quiet dinner with my mom if I was lucky.

Envy twisted up with gratitude at the way they'd welcomed me in here, and I questioned doing the job interview for the five thousandth time this month.

"Over here," Coop murmured, tapping my shoulder before leading me over to two of the empty chairs that had been pulled out, not far from Gramps. Cooper was throwing me for a loop. I'd spent years mouthing off to him, but the second he turned his attention my way, I'd pretty much been reduced to a puddle. A very horny puddle.

This wasn't the time or place though. Not like I could straddle him on the chair in the middle of the family function.

I settled into the beat-up chair closest to Gramps, who stared at me and then his grandson. "Hey, old man," I said, needing to distract him any way possible. "You all ready to come back to work?"

"Beyond ready," he said, pointing down to his boot. "I'm past the crutches point, so I'll be able to zoom around the store."

"No you won't," Coop's mom called over. "You're going to be careful."

"So, backflips, right?" I said, snapping into the usual flow of conversation between me and Gramps, even with the obvious shift of Coop sitting next to me and not scowling for once.

"Don't encourage him," Coop muttered at me. "He'll take you seriously."

I spoke too soon, though the sight of him shaking his head at me filled me with warmth. All too easily I could imagine us here as a couple, me teasing him like usual, him rolling his eyes at me. My heart thundered as my mind soared faster than I could rein it back. The yearning grew so intense it hurt my teeth, the longing I'd been shoving down and trying to ignore for years.

A scrap of attention from Coop, and I was already smitten, which made sense with the amount of time and energy I'd put into annoying him over the years. It was idiotic to think my heart wouldn't get involved.

Only time would tell if he'd be the one to shatter it.

Chapter Thirteen

Cooper

Having Logan dangling within reach all night and not being able to kiss the fuck out of him was torture.

He looked fine as hell, clean-shaven with his crisp scent wafting in my direction. His jeans might as well have been glued to him, his round ass on clear display, and the warm glow in his dark brown eyes whenever he looked at me was so addictive. I was used to Logan smirking, Logan teasing, Logan doing everything within his power to drive me crazy.

Now he drove me crazy in an entirely different way.

Most of my family had cleared out about an hour ago, and Jordan's friends had begun to arrive. With them would be the drinking, the chaos, and more headaches than my niece and nephew brought, since they were a responsible six and eight.

I leaned back in the chair I'd claimed a while ago, my fingers tapping on the edge of it as Jordan's roommate Hal blared on in my ear about some piece-of-shit car he was trying to fix. Don't get me wrong, I could deep dive on a subject with the best of them, but cars weren't my thing. And besides, at some point, Logan had wandered to the opposite side of the room, and the distance was driving me nuts.

We hadn't talked enough to figure out how to act in front of my family—hell, we hadn't even been able to get together again to fuck—but I hadn't been able to help putting my hands all over him the second he showed up. He'd been on my mind nonstop since the other day, and after years of wanting Logan Nichols to leave me the fuck alone, it was an odd experience being on the opposite end of the spectrum. I wanted his attention on me all the time—those blushes, the moans, the little slips of vulnerability I'd been able to coax out of him.

"You should've seen the paint job on this beauty," Hal continued, and I bobbed my head in agreement, only half paying attention.

Logan stood next to Jordan's slender, tattooed friend Rogue—which, who had a ridiculous name like Rogue anyway? The guy was leaning in fucking close though, and my nerves prickled at a slow simmer as the two of them talked. Logan wasn't mine. We hadn't gotten so far as to say more than we wanted to see how this thing between us played out, but my body already reacted on instinct, like he was.

Like he'd always been.

Rogue leaned in again, this time to whisper something in Logan's ear, and he reached out to touch his forearm. My gut curled in on itself.

"I'll be right back," I said, interrupting Hal. I rose from my chair, and my legs moved of their own volition, carrying me in the direction of Logan. My blood was pumping hard, and common sense had escaped out the backdoor, but something about this man had always made me lose my head in a way no one else could manage.

When I stopped in front of them, Logan looked up at me, his eyes widened in surprise. Rogue's brows drew together, like he'd figured out I'd arrived to interrupt them.

"Do you have a second?" I asked Logan, placing a hand on his arm.

He scanned me from head to foot before licking his lips. "Yeah," he responded, his eyes twinkling. "Sorry, Rogue. We'll catch up."

Before Jordan's stupid friend could say anything else, I slipped my hand in Logan's and headed out of the living room. Jordan's backyard was miles of open land, and most of his friends and my siblings were all crammed in the front yard for a game of beer pong. I detoured through the kitchen, not even giving a damn if a few of his friends saw me tugging Logan along.

Honestly, if we'd had five seconds to gauge where we stood, I would've told my family, because secrets didn't stay that way long around here. However, we hadn't even gotten the breathing room to see each other alone since the other day.

The nighttime air was bracing, but it didn't do a thing to cool my blood, pumping hotter and hotter by the second. No one was on the back porch, and I tugged Logan along with me as we stepped as far away from the door as possible, on the other side of the house.

"Did something happen?" Logan asked, a little breathless as I came to a sudden stop.

I whipped around to face him. Those big brown eyes were wide with concern, his lips full and fucking luscious. I'd been going out of my mind all night with the desire to touch him, to savor him, to hear him moan against my mouth again. Before I could rein myself in, I wrapped my hand around the back of his neck and closed the space between us.

Relief washed through me when our lips met, with an intensity that surprised me. The electricity that pulsed through my veins as I savored his mouth was so high voltage I couldn't forget it. Part of me had wondered if I'd only conjured up the force of the connection between us since it had been such a shock to the system, but kissing him again confirmed it. I'd never experienced chemistry like this—a wildfire threatening to raze everything I'd known.

Logan sagged into my arms, like he was equally as affected, and I slipped my arms around his waist to hold him upright. He pressed up against me, a breathy little moan escaping when we pulled away for a moment. God, I wanted that sound on replay over and over again. I could feel the stiffness of his erection against my thigh, and I nudged against it, loving the whimper I got in response. I traced his lips with the tip of my tongue, enjoying the curve of them before I dipped in again to consume him.

He tasted sweet, like the wine he'd been drinking tonight, and I was addicted. I drove my tongue in his mouth, loving how he writhed against me. Logan was so responsive, and all the playfulness he wielded every day turned explosive when he kissed. He wasn't some passive thing in my arms—no, he lapped into my mouth hungrily, only to draw back a moment later to nip at my lip. The way he left me guessing was addictive, a puzzle I needed to solve.

The pounding need hadn't dissipated with having him in my arms, but the thread of anxiety that had been stretching me thinner and thinner did.

I slid my hand up beneath his shirt, feeling the velvet skin of his back. God, I wanted to get him splayed out on my bed so I could taste every inch of him. Our brief interlude in the bookstore hadn't been nearly enough.

Logan drew back an inch, his hot breaths puffing against my lips.

Seeing his eyes all wild like this, his tamed strands rumpled sent me into overdrive. I needed this man right fucking now.

"Please," he moaned out, grinding against my thigh.

We were in Jordan's backyard, a full-fledged party raging on inside, and anyone could come out here at any second and spot us. Hell, my siblings were all here, wandering through the place. And yet, the only thing that mattered right now was Logan's pretty plea and the sheer overdose of lust I got from his proximity alone.

I reached for the button of his jeans. "This what you want?"

He bobbed his head, and I hooked my finger inside the waistband to drag him closer. I took a few steps back until I reached the wall and drew him in front of me. Anyone looking from the door would see my backside. In a few quick movements, I had his button unsnapped and his zipper down.

"Take your cock out," I murmured, keeping my voice low.

His eyes flared with lust as he met my gaze, and he nodded before following directions. I was already unbuckling my belt, the jangle a little too loud in the quiet night. We couldn't make noise—not with people just in the house, and even the slight sounds made me hyperaware that I prepared to fuck around with Logan outside...while an entire party was happening inside.

This wasn't me. I was the careful one, the serious one, the responsible one.

Not the risk-taker. Not impulsive.

And yet something about Logan pushed me past my comfort zone, had me stepping beyond it. He drew out his dick, which I'd barely gotten a glimpse of last time, and I pressed my teeth into my lower lip. Fuck, long and slender with a nice flushed head, he had a goddamn gorgeous cock.

I unzipped my Wranglers and drew my cock from my boxer briefs, trying to keep everything in place as much as possible. Pre-cum leaked at my tip, my length hard as hell from just making out with him. Logan had me keyed up so badly, and I wanted to feel him pressed against me.

"C'mere, beautiful," I said, grabbing his hip and drawing him in closer. Our cocks brushed against each other, and a sinful ripple glided up my spine at the feeling. I spat on my hand and then wrapped it around both of our erections. Leaning in, I nipped at Logan's lower lip. I was rewarded by a shuddery little sigh from him, and he reached up to grip tight to my shirt, letting me take control.

I never would've expected how he melted against me every time. Given how mouthy he'd always been with me, I thought everything with him would've been a fight. But no, Logan surrendered to me with a sweetness he didn't show the rest of the world. And I was fast becoming addicted.

I began to jerk both of us off, dragging some pre-cum from our heads to ease the way. My hand wrapped around our cocks without an issue, and the feel of his velvet length against mine was sin incarnate. I wrapped my other hand around his hip, just to keep him pinned in place while I picked up speed.

The crisp scent of a Wyoming night flooded my senses, mingling with sweat and salt from the pre-cum. While part of me wanted to drop to my knees and take the taste I'd never gotten of Logan, I knew we didn't have that kind of time. Instead, I continued to stroke our cocks, increasing the pace as our hushed breaths cut through the aching quiet out here.

Logan leaned in first, his lips brushing against mine, and I dove right in. Within seconds, we were making out again, his mouth on mine, his tongue slipping in while I jacked us both off. The glide of our pre-cum and the feel of his cock sliding against mine got me so hot I was going to come far too fast. It didn't help that I'd been buzzing with the need for another round with him ever since the first one. Logan was a craving I hadn't gotten enough of.

I drove my tongue into his mouth as the sounds of my hand dragging over our cocks reached my ears, pure fucking music. It felt so damn good, and my lashes fluttered as my balls began to draw up.

Logan's lips were so soft, and he tasted delicious. I could kiss him for fucking hours, but add in the pleasure that rolled through me in crests with each pass of my hand and I was getting closer, closer, closer.

Logan's whole body tensed against mine.

I swallowed down his moans as he came, his cock pulsing jets of cum over my hand. I didn't stop once, continuing to stroke him through it. His cum made the glide even easier, and within seconds, I followed him over the edge.

My balls drew up, and my release rocketed through me with enough intensity that I was gasping against his mouth. Bliss stole me in a mind-blowing wave as my cum mingled with his, soaking my hand. I still stroked us, the cum beginning to squelch between my fingertips. Logan's breaths were ragged, and he licked into my mouth to draw me into a sweet kiss. I tipped my forehead against his, my shoulders heaving as I slowed my strokes.

Sweat prickled on our foreheads, and our breaths commingled as we both came down from the high of our releases. I didn't want to budge from here, but the cum was beginning to drip onto the cement. I should feel guilty about coming on Jordan's back porch, but given the guys he lived with, I was sure this back porch had seen a lot worse.

"We should move, right?" Logan murmured, clutching my shirt loosely. I loved the contact, the way we'd just exploded, same as the first time. However, the cum was starting to cool on my hand, and I needed to wipe it off.

"Yeah." I bit out a reluctant sigh as I pulled away and cut the quick few steps over to the grass. I smeared my hands against the ground, the grass cool against my fingertips. They were still slightly sticky, but it would do until I hit the bathroom. Once I rose from my crouch, Logan was tucking himself away.

Regret pulsed through me. I wanted the chance to enjoy his body for hours, to get him spread across my bed and savor every inch. Hell, I just wanted the chance to spend time with him, to get to know him better because all my past perceptions of him had been dead wrong. My chest squeezed tight. As much as this shift had been sudden, I was fast realizing I needed more of Logan in my life.

I hadn't taken a step forward when the back door suddenly swung open.

Adrenaline burst through me. My hands shot down to my zipper, and I slid my cock in to my boxer-briefs before zipping up. When I glanced over to the door, Jordan was walking in our direction. I licked my lips, wondering if he'd be able to smell the spunk and sweat in the air out here.

"The party's out front, guys," Jordan called over, even as he didn't stop heading our way. "You're missing out on an epic game of beer pong."

"Beer pong and epic don't belong in the same sentence," I responded dryly, trying to ignore the slight tackiness on my palms as I tucked one into my jeans pocket. I stepped beside Logan again, not wanting to just come and ditch, even though my brother had arrived to ruin the afterglow. Seemed apropos of my family though.

Jordan's eyes narrowed as he glanced between us.

I resisted the urge to run my fingers through my hair or smooth down my shirt, which was still rumpled.

Fuck, the cum stain on the deck.

I definitely hadn't gotten the chance to clean it up. Nothing said happy birthday like jizz on your deck.

"Forget your stick-in-the-mud brother," Logan said, stepping past me as he walked up to Jordan. He didn't look my way, but I had the feeling he was running interference. "Let's go play some beer pong."

"That's the spirit," Jordan said, clapping a hand on his back. He glanced to me. "Come on, Coop. Stop brooding outside."

"You guys go ahead," I said, staring off into the backyard. "I just wanted a few more seconds away from all the noise." At least that was somewhat believable. Most of my siblings were loud extroverts, and I was one of the few quiet ones.

Jordan shrugged, and he and Logan walked into the house. The second the door shut, I spun around and scrubbed at the splotch of cum with my shoe, trying to help it blend in with the concrete. I needed to sneak back out here and clean it up, but I could handle the mess before I left. As long as the puddle of cum wasn't openly visible. I nabbed one of the nearby chairs and moved it so one leg covered it.

That would have to do for now.

I slipped inside, making an immediate detour to the bathroom to wash my hands. Once I stepped out, I followed the bulk of the sound toward the front of the house, where Jordan had dragged Logan off for beer pong. I couldn't seem to stay away from Logan if I tried. A huge contrast to a mere month ago when all I wanted was the opposite.

Sadie was at the table, along with Hal, a few of Jordan's friends, and somehow Henry had gotten roped in. Logan stood back watching, Jordan by his side. When he looked up and caught my gaze, I tilted my head toward the coolers of beer off to the side of the house.

He gave a slight nod before stepping in that direction. Adrenaline thrummed through me, but whether it was from getting disrupted or the jolt that coursed through my veins whenever he was around, I wasn't sure. For years, I'd mistaken the feeling as annoyance, but the truth was, the man had the unique ability to elevate my heart rate.

I dipped down to grab a beer at the same time as him on purpose, our hands brushing together. His lips curled into a feline grin as our eyes met. When I straightened back up, I inched in closer to him.

"All this dodging around is hell," I muttered. "The second we get a chance, I'm taking you out on an actual date."

Logan's eyes widened.

Well, now I felt like a dick. Granted, it wasn't like I'd sent out the best signals by jumping on him any second we were in close proximity.

I reached over to run my hand down his back. "Hey, I'm not fucking around here. I might have bad impulse control around you, but I want to explore the chemistry between us, and that means everything."

"You're trouble, Cooper Ellis," he murmured, chewing on his reddened lower lip. Fuck, I wanted to suck it back into my mouth. I needed to step away before I flat-out mauled him all over again. I ran my hand along his back one more time before I let go, even if it wasn't what I wanted.

Logan crooked an eyebrow. "Were you trying to dry your cum hand on my back?"

A laugh slipped out from me, and I thwacked him in the arm. "No, you dick. I dealt with that and the stain out back."

"Oh thank fuck," Logan breathed out. "I was trying to hustle your brother out, hoping you'd catch the memo." His eyes twinkled when they met mine, and I sucked in a breath at how damn different he appeared to me now. I'd seen him a million times in the past, but I'd never really *seen* him.

"I'm serious though," I said. "You and me. A real date. We'll get it on the schedule."

"I'd settle for just getting dicked down," he mumbled.

The thought traveled right to my cock. God, I wanted to drive into his perfect ass so badly, but I wasn't letting him pivot. "You're not getting out of this, Logan Nichols. If we're giving us a go, then you better bet I'm going to treat you right."

"Ew," he murmured with a bratty little grin. A second later though, his eyes softened. "Giving us a go?"

I nodded and reached up to brush my thumb against his chin. If my siblings wanted to interrogate me later, they fucking could. "Yep. I'm serious."

"You're always serious," he teased, but those deflections didn't bother me like they used to. Because I could see clearly now the way his features lit up despite his mile-high defenses.

And more than anything, I wanted to be the one who broke through them.

Chapter Fourteen

Logan

G ramps was coming back to work this week, and I should've been excited. He was one of my favorite people on the planet, and this place felt off without his boisterous presence.

And yet, Coop's last day at his few-week stint at Ellis Books was today, and that had my heart careening all over the place.

Because in a few short weeks, things between us had changed more than I would've believed possible. Daydreamed about, sure, but the part of me that had always been a realist understood Cooper Ellis wouldn't want me. Hell, no one seemed to—not for long.

Except now he was texting me every day and dropping by the shop when I was working to bring me lunch—boyfriend shit on steroids. Because I'd never had a boyfriend who'd been so considerate, and I wasn't even sure if we were dropping the b word or not. Our date was scheduled for this upcoming weekend, which was the one thing keeping me from believing this would all crumble the second he stopped working here.

I leaned back in my seat at the shop, taking a second to glance at my open laptop. My inbox remained empty, and part of me was relieved by that. My bank account, on the other hand, wasn't so thrilled. And

Aunt Beth had been getting more and more nitpicky as of late, even though we barely saw each other. Comments about how I filled the dishwasher, left a towel out in the bathroom, etc. I was well aware it wasn't my home and tried to make myself as unobtrusive as possible, but I needed to get out and soon.

My gaze slipped to the door for the thousandth time in the past half hour. It was close to the time Coop would be showing up for his final shift, and my skin buzzed with anticipation at seeing him again. At Jordan's party, he'd surprised me by all but dragging me outside, kissing me senseless, and then frotting me stupid, but I wasn't complaining in the slightest. He had almost seemed jealous of Rogue when we'd been talking, and that sent a silent thrill through me.

I'd been wanting Coop's eyes on me for years, and goddamn. The man was everything I'd imagined, which terrified me more. Because once he got sick of my shit—everyone did—the loss would be brutal.

The door jingled as it swung open, and I all but swallowed my tongue. After years of seeing Coop around this town, I should be immune to how hot he was, but apparently that wasn't possible. Because capital F fuck, the man looked stupidly gorgeous. He walked in with those Wranglers hugging his thick thighs and the flannel shirt he wore stretched across his broad chest. His thick brows and serious expression always made him look a little growly, but after experiencing all that firsthand, I could say I didn't mind in the slightest.

His gorgeous blues landed on me, and the way they softened had my heart careening all over the place. Cooper Ellis couldn't walk in there fixing me with those looks and expect me to function for the next hour of my shift.

"Ready for your last day?" I called out, needing to detour out of deep-feels territory.

Coop headed straight for me, and I swallowed hard, my mouth dry. The second he saw through my bullshit, all my normal maneuvers failed me. Because something about this man had made me melt even back in high school. It might've been his loyalty or how he took care of his family, watching out for all his younger siblings, but I'd been drawn to him from the start.

He stopped right in front of the desk and leaned over to brush a kiss to my lips. Every time I'd seen him since Jordan's party, he'd greeted me with a kiss, and fuck, I died every time. I nipped at his lower lip before driving my tongue in, turning the kiss a little filthy. My cock was already getting hard though, and any second a customer could come walking in.

Coop pulled back first, a subtle grin on his lips. "My last day after two whole weeks of work. It's about time I got back to my shop anyway."

"Well, I got you a going-away gift, so you'll just have to deal," I said, reaching under the desk for the bag as well as the single cupcake I'd picked up on the way here from Potts Bakery. When I set it in front of him, he eyed it for a second.

"The cupcake's not poisoned, right?" he asked.

I glared at him until I caught the crinkle in his eyes. "Is that Cooper Ellis making a joke? I didn't think it was possible."

"Well, now I know the cupcake is poisoned," he said, cracking open the plastic shell around it. He pursed his lips. "Peanut butter and chocolate?" His gaze softened toward me, and the sheer sweetness the man levied my way would make me turn into a puddle in this seat. I needed to take the reins back.

"You're supposed to eat the cupcake, not me," I warned, a grin curling my lips. "Though if we were off the clock, I wouldn't be opposed."

"What if I want both?" Coop asked, crooking an eyebrow. He dipped his finger into the frosting and lifted the scoop toward my lips. I tilted forward on automatic, lapping at his finger with small licks to tease, enjoying the sweetness of the chocolate ganache. His pupils were blown, but he simply kept his hand steady as I sucked on his finger, locking my gaze with his the entire time. With the bulge in my pants, people would think I was trying to smuggle a hardback out.

I gave his finger one last hearty suck before pulling back. "Look, now your cupcake's ruined."

"Ruin it all you like," he said, his voice husky as hell.

"Stop it," I hissed.

His lips quirked in one hell of a sexy smile as he lifted the cupcake and took a bite. Coop didn't speak for a moment as he savored it, and I watched the entire thing because the bob of his Adam's apple when he swallowed was free porn. He licked his lips nice and slow, and I shifted in my seat. The rest of my workday was going to be hell.

"Delicious," he said in that low, sexy voice of his. Lust rushed through me, and I was all but panting at this point.

The bell tinkled when the door creaked open, splashing cold water over our moment.

I sat straight, refusing to move from my spot behind the desk, lest I offend anyone with the massive hard-on I was packing.

"Both boys working today?" Ms. Hendricks called out. "How did I get so lucky?"

"Perfect timing," Coop said, his voice rich and smooth, the husky rasp from moments earlier nowhere to be found. Fucking bastard. Of course he'd get me all worked up and be able to switch things off while I sat here squirming. The man ticked a lot of Dom boxes, if I were being honest, but that would just be...nngh.

"I'm here to pick up my Tessa Fairbanks fix," Ms. Hendricks said, sweeping over to the stand where the author's books were front and center in the romance category.

"I heard the latest was phenomenal," I commented. The new releases were my babies while I left Gramps to his dusty treasures, and I loved curating not only what was trending but books that were a bit ahead of their times and would fit the reading tastes of folks around town. The focus shift started calming my stupid erection down, but of course Coop perched on the edge of the desk, his ass within grabbing reach.

"She knocks it out of the park every time," Ms. Hendricks said, approaching with her book and setting it on the desk. Her gaze drifted to the half-eaten cupcake. "Celebration?"

"Coop's last day," I explained with a jerk of my thumb in his direction. "Gramps is coming back this weekend."

Her brows drew together. "Is that a good idea?"

I cast her a knowing look. "You try to stop him. I'm making sure he's only on light duty. No hauling books or reshelving anything when he returns."

"We'll be checking in on him," Coop reassured.

Ms. Hendricks passed over her card, and I made quick work of ringing her up and placing the book into the thin paper bag.

"I can swing by too," Ms. Hendricks said. "You're still young. I'm sure you boys have better things to do on your weekends."

Mmm, I had one big thing on my to-do list this weekend, and that was my date with Coop that better end with his dick in my ass—or else I'd riot.

"Gramps would enjoy the company," Coop said, all smooth and sweet like always. Even though he was quieter than most of his family, he was charming as fuck and had won over most of the town.

Ms. Hendricks lifted her bag. "Thank you, boys. I'll tell you what I think about the book, Logan. I don't know what I would do without your recommendations."

Guilt pummeled me at the comment, because fuck, I loved this. Tessa Fairbanks was an indie author who was making splashes, but a lot of the big box stores hadn't picked her up. I'd stocked her in Ellis Books because readers like Ms. Hendricks would adore her. Except if I got the remote job, all of that would end.

"See you soon," I called out, realizing I'd been quiet a little too long. She'd made it halfway across the store, so she just lifted her hand to wave. The door opened and closed as she exited, and my attention zeroed right in on Coop. I nudged the bag in his direction. "You never opened your last-day gift."

Coop shook his head, a slight grin tugging his lips. He reached into the bag and pulled out the latest thriller by Michael Owens. I'd noticed him reading them before, and he'd spent extra time around those books at the store.

"Not sure if you already picked it up," I started, trailing off when he pinned me with his intense gaze.

"Considering it comes out tomorrow, no," he said, reaching forward to run his thumb across my lower lip. He leaned down and replaced his thumb with his lips in a sweet-as-fuck kiss that I savored. My lashes fluttered, and I all but sighed into his mouth as the kiss sent a slow trickle of pleasure down my spine.

Coop pulled back. "Thank you." The seriousness in his tone reached right inside me, which was why this man had always been dangerous. I might be able to play flippant around most, but when Coop wasn't fixing his grumpiness my way, something about him disarmed me.

"Don't thank me," I responded, trying to ignore the way my heart slammed hard. "You haven't found the note in it yet."

Coop flipped the page open to the piece of paper sticking out of the top, and he read it aloud. "So you *can* read. Congratulations, signed Logan." He gave me a sexy eyebrow arch again. "Couldn't help yourself, could you?"

I offered an extra-broad grin. "It wouldn't be me if I didn't antagonize you."

He clutched his chest. "Don't know how I would live without your taunts."

My gaze drifted to the clock—hell, only fifteen minutes before my shift ended. Sad part was, I didn't want to leave. Granted, the more time Coop and I spent in close proximity, the harder it would be to keep from finding a dark corner and blowing each other, since that seemed to be our trend.

"At least your life's about to get a lot easier after today, down to two jobs again," I said, breaking through the quiet that had descended. His three-job juggle had made it nigh impossible for us to get together, and the idea of more time on the horizon with Coop was everything I'd dreamed of.

The silence stretched out between us, a heaviness to it that had me looking his way. Coop's lips were pressed in a thin line, his eyes stormy. I gnawed on my lower lip. What had I said? Before then, our conversation had flowed, nice and easy. The last two times I'd mentioned jobs he'd gotten tetchy too. While I probably should leave well enough alone, I couldn't help the words that burst out of my mouth.

"Is everything okay with the leatherworking business?"

Coop's eyes flashed in surprise. His brows furrowed on instinct as he reverted back to a far-too-familiar expression. "Did Kai tell you?"

My chest squeezed tight. Apparently it was a sensitive topic. "Nah, I just pay attention."

Coop leaned his full weight against the desk, all but sagging into it. He skimmed his fingers through his thick hair and let out a helpless little noise that tied my heart in knots.

"The business is failing," he murmured, his voice so quiet I almost missed it. For once, I kept my damn mouth shut, realizing Coop opening up was a rare as hell thing. "The bills are rolling in, but the orders have dried up, and the out-of-towners aren't buying enough to fill in the gaps."

I chewed on my lower lip, biting back the urge to offer suggestions. Folks didn't always take kindly to them, and Coop was as stubborn as they came. When I'd arrived at Ellis Books, Gramps barely broke even each month. But we'd done work to the socials, to update the inventory, to reach the customers, and now business was booming.

"I'm sorry," I said. "That fucking blows. Having the craft active in town is important, and I wish people were seeing that."

He stared at the ceiling. "I feel like I'm letting Uncle Ray down."

Fuck. I remember when the Ellis family lost Ray—the accident had rocked them. My throat grew tight at witnessing this side of Coop. In all the time I'd known him, I'd never seen him be vulnerable with any-one—not with friends, not with folks around town, not with family. He was always the rock, the fixer, the one who everyone else went to with their problems.

I reached over for his hand and squeezed. "Hey," I said, my voice coming out low. "Ray would just be proud of you for keeping the craft alive, whether you make a business out of it or not."

His gaze swept my way, the depth in those blue eyes holding me hostage. His tongue darted out to glide over his lower lip. "Thanks, Lo. I think I needed to hear that." He drew his stare away to scan over the bookstore. "Fuck, if I had any sort of social media savvy, maybe I could pull myself out of this rut, but I've been taking on more and more handyman jobs around town instead. Honestly, working at the bookstore has been a reprieve from thinking about my problems."

The opening was right there—fuck it. "You know who does have social media savvy?" I caught his gaze and fluttered my lashes. His brows drew together, the line between them deepening. "This bitch."

"I'm not going to take advantage of you," Coop insisted, the oh-so-familiar crossed-arms posture returning.

"Well, I did have a whole idea of sexy payments in mind, but alternately, I could work on commission," I said, speaking before I processed what I'd volunteered to do. How the hell I was going to manage that with a new gig was beyond me. This job had a lot of downtime even with the new initiatives I'd started here, so I'd been able to work on editing jobs, tool around with some side income for myself. But the remote work would be nonstop.

All of my passions would pretty much get flushed down the drain.

Coop let out a light huff. "We haven't even gone on our first date," he said, and I resisted the urge to reach up and try to smooth out the line between his brows. "I don't want you thinking I'm just dating you for your marketing skills."

"Let's be honest, you're dating me for this," I said, pointing to my fabulous backside.

"While you're hot as hell, that's not the only reason," he said, ruining my attempts at flippant with all his seriousness.

I rolled my eyes. "Why can't I get you to objectify me?"

"Oh, I'll do that plenty," he said, his voice dropping into the sexy tone that pretty much had a direct line to my cock. His gaze slipped past me. "Though, it's the end of your shift, so I'll have to do that next time I see you."

My chest sank at the realization, and I pushed myself up from the desk, starting to get my laptop in order and gather my things. He settled into the seat, passing me a heated look and spreading those legs as he settled in comfortably, which was inviting as sin.

"I'll see you soon," I said, hooking my laptop bag over my shoulder.

"At our date," Coop corrected, crooking a finger to me. I leaned in to press a kiss to his lips, letting the shiver of pleasure at the contact bolster me.

I reluctantly pulled back and tugged at the strap of my laptop bag again. "See you then," I said before I turned on my heel and headed for the door.

The time flew whenever I was around him, and I couldn't seem to get enough. As much as I tried to take this step by step, my heart was tumbling forward faster than intended, like I'd tripped and was rolling my way down a hill. The adrenaline rush was like nothing else—giddy, thrilling, eye-opening—and yet, I hoped when I finally stopped tumbling, I wouldn't be crashing onto jagged rocks.

Chapter Fifteen

Cooper

M y date with Logan was tomorrow, but it couldn't come fast enough.

All we'd been getting were these slices of time, brief moments that weren't nearly enough. Sitting here in my quiet leatherworking shop was making my skin crawl too. I'd gotten caught up on my orders for the week a few days ago, and I no longer had the bookshop to distract me. The desire to play around with a new leatherworking project hadn't been striking like it used to, ever since the bills started stacking up higher and higher.

I skimmed over the invoices for the thousandth time and then wrinkled my nose. I'd looked at different social media all day today, but it was a foreign language to me. And I didn't understand how marketing to the people who knew I was here would help. Uncle Ray's old contacts had lasted me a few years, but when certain local ranchers sold their businesses, I'd reached the point I was at now.

Normally, I would've never confided in anyone like I had Logan—and in the past, never him. For years, I thought he had the upper hand between us, the ability to irritate me like no one else. However, the moment I realized that wasn't the truth, my entire perspective shifted. No, once I saw outside of my tunnel vision, the raw attraction, the emotion Logan had been hiding behind jabs for years broadcasted clear as day.

A shadow fell over the windowpane in the front door of my shop, and I glanced up. I wasn't expecting any visitors, but I got the occasional drop-in to place an order. Maybe I should have made my place a bit more approachable, but half the time I wasn't here, out on handyman jobs, so it wasn't like a storefront where I was accessible at all hours.

The door creaked open, and the very guy I'd been thinking about stepped into view.

Logan looked fucking edible.

His thick blond strands drifted across his forehead, escaping the style he'd attempted to force them into, and the simple black tee he wore stretched across his pecs, highlighting the slender frame I'd felt crushed against mine. With his sharp nose, big brown eyes, and angular jawline, he'd always drawn attention. Truth be told, he'd always attracted mine, but we'd spent so much of the time bickering that I'd confused those feelings along the way.

Fuck, I'd had his lips on mine just yesterday, but already, I wanted to kiss him senseless all over again.

"Lock the door and come over here," I said, tapping on the edge of the desk in front of me.

Logan lifted an eyebrow. "Oh yeah?" He reached behind him to flip the latch on the door. Not like anyone else had walked in today.

I cleared the papers to the side, making my intention crystal clear.

He lifted the bag in his hand. "But what about the dinner I brought?"

"Fuck, it can wait," I all but growled. I didn't know what about Logan made me lose my mind, but the second he entered my proximity, his nearness scrambled my senses. Clearly, the sniping we'd done through the years had been the world's best foreplay, because now I couldn't help but dive headfirst into the sexual tension that erupted between us whenever we were in the same room.

A smirk rolled to his lips, and he took his time sauntering over, making sure to swing his hips as he went. He leaned to place the bag of dinner down on the floor by the side of my desk, dipping nice and low. His ass popped in those tight-as-hell jeans, and I salivated at the sight. I'd been thinking about those pert cheeks for an eon now, and ever since we'd cracked the Pandora's box open between us, the need to dive between them, however possible, had risen to a roaring crescendo.

"Something you want?" Logan said as he glanced over to catch me watching him straighten up.

"Hell yeah," I said, spreading my legs to make room for him. "You want to thrust your ass like that? Get right in front of me then, hands on the desk."

He blinked for a moment, as if shocked by my directness. Logan might have paid more attention to me than I realized in the past, but he'd never seen me behind closed doors. And with him, I could barely seem to even keep things to closed doors. He unleashed a wildness in me that had been missing from every other hookup, date, or partner.

"What are you waiting for, beautiful?" I leaned back in my chair.

"Fuck," he swore. "I want to make you work for it, but I've been out-of-my-mind horny." He stepped in front of me and spun to face the desk, his hands landing on the top with a slap. When he bent over so his perfect ass was right in front of me, I couldn't help but reach out and stroke the surface through the denim. "You can spank it if you want," he said, glancing back.

I crooked a brow. "Oh, is that what you like?"

"The more pain the better," he said, his dark eyes sparkling. My cock throbbed in response. I hadn't played hard with a lot of my partners in the past, but the porn I tended to gravitate toward was always of the kink variety. Logan gave an up-nod to some of the equestrian supplies I had laid out on the far desk. "Like those paddles? They'd give a delicious slap."

I licked my lips, all the oxygen sucked up from the room. The idea of his pretty cheeks all red from a paddling, getting to feel the satisfying thwack of the leather with each strike—fucking headrush. No one had ever suggested integrating my leather into the bedroom before, even if I'd been curious for a long while. But Logan had been unique in every regard. I ran my palm across his backside again.

"What's your safeword?" I asked. If we were going to play, even lightly, I needed us to be on the same page.

"I prefer the stoplight system, if you're familiar," Logan said.

"Green for all clear, yellow for near the edge, red for stop," I repeated. "I don't have as much practical experience with impact play, so you'll have to speak up if anything feels off." I rose from my perfect view reluctantly, but the feeling was replaced by a thunderbolt of adrenaline the moment I lifted the leather paddle from the stack. The broad heft of it was nice and heavy, and the leather was supple and smelled delicious. God, the thrill that rippled up my spine as I approached Logan with it in my hand was unreal. His nostrils flared, and the heat cranked up about a hundred degrees hotter.

"If this is your first time, just go until the cheeks are nice and red, an even color," Logan said. "Keep the strikes to the meaty sections—my ass can take it."

Fuck, this man. I reached down to adjust my aching cock in my jeans. This was a fantasy I hadn't ever thought I'd get to experience, and I was well aware Logan Nichols was the one fulfilling it. He'd delivered surprise after surprise, and I couldn't wait to keep finding out more—starting with the pretty noises he made when I paddled that pert ass.

I stepped behind him again, reaching around to unbuckle his belt with a jangle. After attacking the button and the zipper on his jeans, I tugged them along with his briefs down to his waist, getting an eyeful of the smooth, delicious skin I wanted to sink my teeth into. Hell, my mouth watered to lap between his cheeks, but that would be so much more rewarding once his cheeks were nice and hot.

I gave a few exploratory smacks of the paddle against my palm to gauge my swing. The sting wasn't too hard but delicious enough to linger. I ran my palm over Logan's ass, loving the whole-body shiver that rippled through him. His cock hung between his legs, all thick and erect, his balls smooth and shaved. The man took care of himself, which only made me want to rim him into oblivion.

First things first.

I lifted my arm and unleashed the first blow. It landed with a delicious thwack that echoed through the room, and Logan's ass bounced with the movement.

"The love tap's cute," he mouthed off, because of course he did. My lips curled with satisfaction at the way he egged me on.

"Glad you think so," I said, this time bringing my arm up before descending with the paddle. This one landed with a sharper crack, and a breath huffed out from Logan, his lashes fluttering.

"Good on you for taking those baby steps." His words made my pulse skyrocket. All the taunting he'd levelled at me for years had never failed to crank my blood pressure up—I'd just never realized why.

"It's almost like you're asking for it, gorgeous," I responded, letting the paddle fly with a satisfying smack. I began to alternate strokes against his cheeks, watching the blush bloom there with each one. The stress melted away from me with each swing, and I had to question why I hadn't tried this far, far sooner. If Logan and I could've been doing this for the last ten years instead of bickering, well, goddamn.

Logan let out a low moan as a harder blow landed.

"Color?" I asked, wanting to check in. As much fun as I was having, I didn't want to do anything to hurt Logan in a negative way.

"So green, babe," he murmured, his words coming out almost in a slur.

I took a step in closer, reaching around him with my other hand to wrap it around his cock.

"Oh god," Logan said, almost keeling forward as I gave his length a few light strokes—mostly to feel the heft in my hand, how hard and dripping he was. His lashes fluttered, and I absorbed every minute reaction from him, even the slight hitch of his breath, the way a small tremble rocked through his whole body. With him splayed forward like this, the curve of his back was sexy as fuck.

I let go of his cock again and stepped away, finding my stance. His ass cheeks were getting to be a rosy color, but they weren't the glowing red I wanted before I continued to enjoy his body.

I brought the paddle down on his ass again, hard enough that he yelped, the thwack echoing through the room. The feel of the leather in my hand and watching him squirm in response had me harder than I think I'd ever gotten before. My cock throbbed with need as it tested the confines of my jeans. The urge to bury myself inside him rose with every strike against his ass, the beautiful way his back arched, and the loud noises he made. Logan had always been expressive as hell, but I'd never realized just how hot that could be.

Fuuuuck, this man was gorgeous in so many different ways.

His cheeks had grown bright red now, and I'd hit the point where I couldn't wait any longer before tasting him. I placed the paddle on the desk beside him with intention and then took a seat in the chair behind him, which set his luscious ass directly in front of me.

"You did so good," I murmured, and the hitch of his breath in response sent a burst of warmth through me. I palmed his cheeks, the heat of them fucking intoxicating. Spreading him open, I leaned in to lap at the center of him, a few exploratory licks. He tasted a little earthy, and his whole posture went slack the moment I began. When I lapped at him again, a low moan escaped. The sound only spurred me on, and I licked a stripe from his balls to his hole. His legs trembled in response, and I ran my hands along those warm cheeks, feeling the blaze of my handiwork before diving back in.

I nipped and sucked at the soft skin there before driving my tongue into his hole. The heat surrounding my face, the velvet of his ass against my palms kept me hard as a rock, and I lost myself in rimming him into oblivion. I gripped his hips to pin him in place as I continued my attack. Saliva dripped down his crack, a few drops slipping to the floor, but I didn't pause in the slightest. Logan wasn't bothering to restrain his moans at this point. He was loud and lusty the way I'd been wanting to hear him, and his responsiveness spurred me on.

He began to shift his hips back, all but riding my face at this point. I drank in the taste of him, loving how he moaned and writhed and moved. The idea of his heat squeezing my cock was enough to make my eyes roll back, but I'd been needing a taste of him for so long that I didn't want to pull away. This fucking ass. It was so damn delicious I could sit here happily for hours.

"Oh god, oh god," Logan burst out. "I'm close."

I reached down and tugged at his balls before giving one last lick to his hole. "You're not coming yet."

Logan managed to glance back, his grin lopsided. "Trying to control my orgasms now too? It's not fair that you're this fucking hot, babe."

"There's no trying about it," I said, giving his cheek a light spank before I pushed up from my seat. "You're going to come on my cock or not at all."

"I've got condoms and lube in the pocket of my jeans," Logan breathed out. "And I'm negative."

"Same." I unzipped my jeans, the sound echoing loud in the room. I didn't bother with his pocket, reaching to the top drawer of my desk.

Logan arched a brow as he glanced back to me. "Dirty, Mr. Ellis. What are you doing with lube at your work desk?"

I gripped his ass hard, and he let out another long, low moan. "Don't know, Lo, what would I be doing with lube at my desk? Stroking myself thinking about mouthy little sluts who need to be dicked down?"

"Nngh." Logan bit his lips, his nostrils flaring. "How have you been keeping this filthy side from me for so many years?"

"We've got a lot of time to make up for," I murmured. I took my cock out and rolled the condom on my length before coating it in a liberal amount of lube. The rest I smeared across his pretty spit-slicked hole. Fuck, this man painted the prettiest picture. Bent over my desk, ass out, and his pants had drifted to his ankles. His blond strands were splayed messily across his forehead, and his dark brown eyes glowed with lust. Those lips were as cherry red as his ass, and the sight of his cheeks with my mark on them made me want to dive in all over again.

Except this time, I'd be driving in with my cock.

I gave myself a slow stroke as I lined up with his hole, unsure if I'd be able to keep from nutting after sinking inside him. Despite the other times we'd fucked, we hadn't done penetrative yet, and the filthy fantasies of it that had been parading through my mind amped up my desire.

I sucked in a deep inhale, the room smelling like sex and leather, which only got me hotter. We'd need more repeats here, because I wanted to fuck him all over my studio. Slowly, I sank inside Logan.

"Fuck, fuck, fuck," he breathed out as I glided in with ease. The vise of his ass was pure heaven. The tight heat wrapped around my cock, and I never wanted to leave. My breaths came in a little faster, and I stayed still for a moment to keep from blowing my load like a goddamn teenager.

I ran my palm against his ass cheek again. "You feel like sin, beautiful."

Logan began to squirm, clearly wanting more. I continued to palm at his ass cheeks, squeezing the firm, heated flesh and enjoying the snug feel of his hole squeezing my cock tight.

"Are you going to fuck me or just play with my ass?" he said, his voice taking on a delicious strained quality that I adored.

"You've got a mighty fine ass to play with," I murmured, amusement creeping into my tone. If this was how he'd felt when he'd tormented me for years, I could understand a smidge why he'd done it. And he'd earned plenty of this in return.

Logan tried to shift his hips back to spear himself deeper on my cock.

"Something you need?" I asked, feigning innocence.

Logan shot a glare to me. "You're doing this on purpose."

"Maybe if you ask sweetly, I'll fuck you nice and hard like you want," I responded, arching a brow. Need simmered through me at this point, and my entire body was one tense wire begging to unleash, but I wouldn't pass up the chance to give Logan a taste of his own medicine.

"Guess neither of us will end up satisfied," Logan shot back. I continued to pinch and touch the abused flesh of his cheeks, loving the way he shifted at each and every touch.

The more I played and didn't move an inch inside this snug bliss, the more Logan fidgeted. I could see how he buzzed, just as close to snapping as I was. But I was determined to hold steady.

Silence stretched between us, so I palmed at his ass, running my hands around his waist, down his back, memorizing every inch of his gorgeous body and the way he looked splayed out and speared on my cock.

"Fine," Logan burst out at last. "Please, Coop, please fuck me."

Warmth curled inside me along with immense satisfaction.

"Hell yes," I growled out, gripping his hips tight. I pulled back and thrust in, and the guttural groan that burst from him was pure sex. The slow, sinuous glide of pleasure intensified as I began to find my pace, rocking in and out of him at a steady rhythm. Each thrust had us both gasping for breath, and sparks were already flying from the smooth glide, from the delicious heat of his ass, from how perfect this felt.

I could fuck Logan Nichols for the rest of my goddamn life.

My grip on his hips tightened, and I slammed home again, my lashes fluttering. After all the playing around, I unleashed. Logan brought his hips back to meet my thrusts, his plush ass bouncing with each impact. My breaths came out heavier, and I lost myself to the frenzy. The slap of skin to skin echoed through the room, along with the jangle of my belt. Sweat dripped down my forehead, and I could already taste the salt in my mouth.

I moved with the ferocity of everything I'd been holding back, a wildness surging through me that I couldn't ignore. My heart thumped so hard I could hear the boom, boom, boom, and my vision blurred as I blinked back sweat. Logan's cries mixed with my own, and I lost myself to the sensations overwhelming me. The tension grew unbearable at this point, the need for release becoming more and more intense. The slide inside him sent sparks traveling up my spine every time I moved, and I couldn't help chasing it again and again and again.

My breaths were coming out heavier, my palms slick with the sweat pooling between us as we collided, all the explosiveness that had been brewing between us for years unleashed.

"God, I've got to come," Logan breathed out, his voice shaking.

My arms trembled, but I rammed into him harder and harder, as if we could somehow merge and become one. The heat of his ass against my skin, the flawless fit of his hole around my cock—I'd never felt this perfection before, and I doubted I would again. My balls were beginning to draw up, and any moment I'd be sailing over the edge. I wanted Logan to fly right along with me.

I reached up to thread my fingers through his hair, giving it a sharp tug even as I continued to thrust inside him, not ceasing for a moment. "Come for me."

As if those words flipped a switch, all of a sudden Logan's hole spasmed around my cock, and a long, guttural moan escaped him as he sagged forward. The motion did me in. Before I was even aware, my orgasm barreled ahead, and I was coming.

My cum shot out of me, and bliss flooded through me in a fucking tidal wave, my limbs trembling. I let myself get dragged away, my vision whiting out for a moment from the intensity of my release.

My breaths were as ragged as Logan's as we both hunched over the desk, my chest to his back, his hands splayed out against the surface.

"Goddamn," I swore, a reverence in my tone that was deserved. The sparks, the chemistry between us was beyond undeniable—we had the potency of a summer storm brewing between us, and each time we collided together left me in complete and utter awe. Slowly, my body descended back to earth, and I absently petted along Logan's side, lingering at his reddened cheeks.

"I think you fucked away my ability to speak," Logan murmured, his voice quaking.

I barely caught the click of the lock at my front door before it went swinging open.

Chapter Sixteen

Logan

My brain was fried from getting the sort of paddling I ached for and then getting rimmed and fucked until I was delirious.

But even my tired-ass brain registered the swing of the door as it opened wide.

"What the hell are you doing with your place locked—" Coop's best friend Kai started as he busted in. The words died off as he looked up at us. "Oh, shit."

Adrenaline raced through me, but I couldn't do anything with Coop balls-deep inside me and all but covering my body with his. Rather than saying anything else, Kai circled around and stepped out the door. The click was audible in the quiet.

Despite the orgasm that had been wrung from me, my heart raced from our surprise visitor, and already my mind was attempting to come back online. Would Coop deny that we were together? I wasn't sure how he would explain away being caught literally inside me, but the idea of it made my stomach churn.

"I regret giving him a key," Coop muttered as he slowly began to pull out. He rested a hand on my ass, which was so tender and blazing at this point. "Do you need aftercare? I can tell Kai to go the hell home."

I shook my head, even though spending time with Coop post-orgasm sounded like bliss. We kept getting interrupted, and while the suddenness of our hookups were hot as hell, at this point I'd give my left nut for the chance to relax in a bed afterwards. "The spanking definitely worked for me, but the play wasn't so intense that I need aftercare. Just maybe give me a few minutes before sending me packing." Even as I said the words, my heart twisted, a little ugliness stirring there.

Coop placed his hands on my shoulders and turned me around. His pants were back up and zipped because it was him. "Lo, if I'd send anyone packing, it'd be Kai. You're not just some cheap fling to me."

My heart expanded a dozen sizes at those words. We hadn't exchanged the b word yet, but he'd made it clear we were dating at the very least. Despite the amount of shit I'd given Coop for being a stick-in-the-mud over the years, his steadfastness was one of his most attractive qualities. Once he made his mind up about something, he wasn't the sort to flake out or shy away.

And god, I'd fantasized for years about all his steadfastness focused my way.

It'd be more than anything I'd experienced from family or boyfriends.

"So, how's Kai going to react to seeing us together?" I asked, trying to pivot into teasing territory. "Is this going to be in his spank bank for the next century?" I managed to get my pants zipped, even though the fabric was scratchy against the tender skin of my ass, and my hands still trembled a bit.

"Nah, Kai's as straight as they come," Coop said, wiping my cum off the surface of his desk with a paper towel. "Though, this is new territory in our friendship. He's never walked in on me before."

I ran my fingers through my hair, as if I could attempt to make it look less like Coop had been tugging on it while fucking me hard. God, I was going to have bruises everywhere tomorrow, and I adored it. "So, what are we going to tell him?"

Coop shook his head as he walked over to the door, tossing the paper towel in the wastebasket as he went. "Kai, you can come back in," he called, yanking the door open.

I didn't bother trying to stand anymore, sinking into the seat behind the desk. My knees were shot to shit from the onslaught of pleasure combined with getting bent over for the extended period of time. God, that was hands down the best sex I'd had in my life. I'd done some kink experimenting, but finding partners around here wasn't the easiest, and it was always better to play with someone you trusted.

The door creaked open, and Kai walked in slowly, giving us quick glances, probably to make sure we were decent. We'd scarred the pretty little straight boy for life.

"So, I've learned a valuable lesson about busting into your studio," Kai said, his lips quirking with a grin. So, maybe not that scarred. "But now I need to know how long this has been going on?"

"It's recent," Coop said, striding back to lean against the desk beside me. His presence soothed me, even though I didn't want to admit it because I hated relying on people. "But we're seeing each other."

My eyebrows rose to my hairline at the casual way Coop announced we were together. This was his best friend, and I'd expected him to give Kai the runaround instead of flat-out admitting we were dating.

Kai blinked and then looked first at me, then at Coop. "I'm guessing this guy finally realized you've had a thing for him for the last century?"

"Took long enough, right?" I teased, Kai's easygoing manner setting me at ease.

Coop scrubbed at his face with his palms. "No, no, no. None of this ganging up on me shit. The two of you get along far too well."

"Isn't that what you'd hope for?" I asked sweetly, batting my lashes. "It's because I'm so likeable."

"Is that what the kids are calling pain in the ass now?" Coop responded, a small smirk tugging at his lips. As much fun as it had been to irritate him in the past, I couldn't deny I enjoyed this so much more now that he bantered back with me.

"I mean, if anyone's the pain in the ass," I said, arching an eyebrow.

"Oh come on," Kai said, slashing at the air. "I've already seen too much."

"And whose fault is that?" Coop shot back. "What were you coming over here for anyway?"

"Another potential gig from one of the ranches I was delivering to," Kai said, reaching into his pocket to pull out a folded paper. "Figured you'd want the lead." He snapped his head up to look at Coop, wrinkling his nose.

Coop heaved out a sigh. "It's fine. Logan knows."

Kai crossed his arms over his chest and stared at me. "Wait, Mr. Keeps to Himself opened up to you? Are you about to get married?"

My heart stumbled. I knew Coop didn't share easily, but hearing Kai's confirmation reminded me. "I was nosy and pieced things together." And part of me had been hoping in stopping by that Coop would let me play around with some of his social media—because it was clear the boy was floundering in that regard. I reached forward for the paddle we'd been playing with before our rude interruption.

The idea descended like a lightning strike.

"Why the hell aren't you selling kink toys?" I blurted out.

Both Kai and Coop turned their stares on me. Then Kai seemed to connect the paddle in my hand to what he'd witnessed, and his eyes widened and his cheeks pinked. My shame had exited stage left the moment Kai had walked in on us right after we'd come. To be fair, I'd never had a lot of it in the first place.

Coop's brows drew together. "Who the hell's going to walk in to buy a flogger?"

I rolled my eyes. "My god, you Luddite. You're somehow worse than Gramps. You have access to the internet and a whole horde of kinksters who'd pay good money for quality leather products."

Coop's jaw dropped, and he stared at me like I'd spoken in tongues.

"Well, shit," Kai said. "I feel like an idiot now."

"You could get a website up and running in no time, and I promise you, you'll have the kink community lining up to order their floggers and paddles from you, or whatever else you want to play around with. Puppy masks? Bridles for pony play?" My mind was running a hundred miles a minute because this was shit I adored. Creative marketing came naturally for me, and I loved applying it to my interests.

Coop rapped his knuckles against the surface of the desk. "You know, sometimes you open your mouth and I want to strangle you, and other times I'm just in awe of how goddamn brilliant you are."

My heart thumped a little harder at the sheer admiration shining in his eyes. He dipped down and pressed an emphatic kiss to my lips. Before I could even register he was kissing me, he'd already pulled back. Coop shook his head, a larger smile than I'd ever seen from him growing on his face.

"Holy fuck, Lo," he murmured. "You fucking genius. I'd never even considered doing anything like that."

"Do you still want this job?" Kai asked, lifting the paper.

Coop snatched it from him. "Yeah, thanks. I need to pay the bills, but hell. The idea of selling kink toys? I think it actually has legs."

The concept definitely did, but Coop needed more time to process. "Lucky for you, you're dating someone who knows how to set up the online business *and* get it in front of the kinky folks who'd be interested."

Coop gave me a firm look. "I'll pay you to set it up. I'm not going to take advantage of you."

"Mm, that could be fun though," I said, waggling my brows.

"Guys, I'm right here," Kai groaned.

"Sorry, voyeurism isn't my kink," I continued. "Though, if that's your thing, there's a host of folks who'd love a willing participant to watch."

Kai shook his head. "Yeah, let me run that one by Shel. I'm sure she'd be thrilled."

"Ugh, vanilla folks," I said with mock disgust.

"Like Kai needs to ruin his perfect relationship." Coop stepped in. "He's got the whole charmed high school sweetheart thing going on."

Kai's expression darkened for a moment before it lightened again. "Definitely don't need a Craigslist weirdo watching us bang."

"Oh god, please don't go trolling on Craigslist," I said, placing a hand over my chest in horror. His reaction had snared my curiosity, but it also wasn't my place to dig. Coop clearly was unaware, but the man wasn't known for his astute nature, given that he'd missed my blatant obsession with him for a goddamn decade. "If you pop up a personals on Craigslist, you're inviting in a horror show."

"Okay," Coop said, grabbing a pen and paper. "I'm writing your idea down—not the Craigslist shit." He started to jot notes onto it, like the adorable technologically deficient person he was.

"You know, most of us just use a notes app on our phone nowadays," I commented, only to earn a glare from Coop.

Kai's nose wrinkled. "The leather hid it at first, but it smells like spunk in here."

"Did you expect anything else after barging in on us?" I asked, settling in the seat and pulling out my phone. Already, I bookmarked a few sites we'd need to look at for competitive pricing while Coop continued on with his adorably simple handwritten list.

He lifted his head, swiping a hand between the two of us. "Stop with the bickering. I'm running out of time here, and I can't wait around on moving forward with this."

I straightened up in my seat and reached over for my laptop bag, which had been leaning against the side of the desk—shockingly not toppled over even after all the movement this thing had received. My heart was thumping hard at the open hope in Coop's eyes, at the way the ideas whirred through my brain.

"Settle in, guys," I said, cracking my laptop and turning it on. "We've got a business to save."

Chapter Seventeen

Cooper

The day of my date with Logan had arrived.

After all the little scraps of time we'd cobbled together, I was craving more in a big way. To spend a whole evening talking, kissing, fucking—whatever—without interruptions. It was hard to believe we hadn't even gone out together yet with how seamlessly I'd fallen into the stride of talking with him, thinking about him constantly.

And tonight was the first chance we'd gotten without jobs and obligations tugging us in opposing directions. Wild how fast I'd gone from wanting to be anywhere else but near him to craving his whiplash smile, the clever mind that always seemed to be at work, and the almost shy way he melted for me—a total contradiction from the cocky front he'd wielded for years.

I just had one stop to make first.

The sign for Ellis Books stood out at the end of the block, an even more familiar beacon for me after spending two weeks helping out at the shop. Except, the place had new memories for me now, ones I never would've anticipated. My chest warmed as I approached the door, a laden bag in my hand. Logan and I had never even had a hard and firm boyfriend talk, but I hoped we could broach that today, because I wanted his attention solely to myself.

The door jangled when I opened it, the scent of leather and old books wafting my way. I dragged in a long, slow breath of it as I scanned the place.

Gramps wasn't sitting behind the desk.

Irritation prickled along my arms. Of course he wasn't where he was supposed to be. Give the man an inch and he'd take the whole ranch. This was his first official day back, and guaranteed he wouldn't be careful and stay in one spot. I understood he was going stir-crazy at home, but if he started scaling the shelves, I was ratting him out to Mom. She'd put him in his place.

"Old man, where are you at?" I called out, walking deeper into the bookstore.

A rattle sounded followed by a thump.

I stepped around one of the bookshelves to stop still. Gramps and Ms. Hendricks were looking mighty rumpled as they moved away from each other. I crossed my arms over my chest, a grin rising to my lips unbidden. Well, damn. Apparently Logan and I weren't the only ones who liked to get frisky between the stacks.

"When did you get here?" Gramps asked, paying close attention to his pocket watch all of a sudden.

"Just now," I responded. "Thought you might need some extra help on your first day back, but I can see Ms. Hendricks has that covered."

A furious blush lit her cheeks, and both of them kept averting their eyes like they were teens.

Holy shit, this was good. Amusement bubbled up in my chest. I couldn't wait to tell Logan and the rest of my family. I was always the last person to hear any gossip going on, so this situation was rare. "Well, I guess I'll leave the early dinner I brought over at your desk."

I strode in that direction and dropped the bag off, giving them a few extra seconds to straighten up.

"Where are you off to?" Ms. Hendricks asked, clearing her throat a little in the process.

"Heading to a date with Logan," I announced, striding toward the door. "Hope you enjoy the rest of your day." I heard a few murmurs behind me, but I didn't turn back. Guaranteed, Gramps and Ms. Hendricks would want to grill me, but I was going to savor having the upper hand here for once. Usually I got dragged into everyone else's messes—it was time I could drop some news of my own for once.

After hopping into my truck, I turned on the ignition and headed in the direction of Jake's.

We'd agreed to meet there to grab takeout, and I had a special spot I wanted to steal him away to, rather than eating inside the bar where we'd get bothered the entire night. Secluded outdoors was about the only chance I'd get to spend time alone with Logan and not share our date with half of our nosy town who'd be prying. My heart thumped a little harder as I slid into a parking spot near Jake's, as if I hadn't seen him in weeks. It might've just been a few days that had passed, but it felt longer—especially with how much I'd been craving this time with him.

I checked my phone as I got out of my truck—fuck, I was here a little earlier than planned. The bar was the next building up, the big signs making it clear even if I'd been at the end of the block.

"Coop?" Logan's voice sounded feet away.

Adrenaline burst through me, and I turned around to face him. I hadn't felt this nervous for a date since I was a teen, but hell, maybe that made sense. After all, we'd been dodging around this tension between us ever since those years.

When I caught sight of Logan, I just about swallowed my tongue. The man always looked sexy as fuck, but he'd stepped up the game tonight. His blond hair was tamed, and the blue button-down he wore clung to his slender torso, making me want to yank the fabric off him. More of those fuck-me peel-off jeans were painted to his legs, and I couldn't wait to get him out of them later.

"Got here early too?" I asked, a grin threatening to break on my face. Fuck, I hadn't smiled this easily in ages, but the second I realized Logan hadn't been tormenting me just to be a dick, it was like a switch flipped. I now recognized all his in-your-face brand of affection that I'd mistaken throughout the years.

"If you never left since last night, is it getting here early?" Logan asked, fighting with his own grin as he approached.

I arched a brow. "Somehow I doubt Rye let you sleep in the bar after closing." We'd been in this position a thousand times before—outside of Jake's, lobbing snarky comments at each other, but now I understood the tension that had been simmering was the need to fuck.

"You're just salty you weren't invited to the twenty-four hour rager," Logan said with a sniff. He came to a stop in front of me, and I didn't hesitate.

I hooked my finger into the waistband of his jeans and dragged him flush against me before claiming his mouth.

Logan tasted sweet, like vanilla, and I drank him in, losing myself into the feel of those plush lips against mine. The sun soaked into my skin as I kissed him out in front of Jake's Tap, in the middle of Collier's Creek. If anyone didn't know we were dating, they would now.

I swept my tongue in, and he let out a slutty little groan that I lapped up. Goddamn, this man was addictive. With his body pressed against mine, my mind was reeling, my heart skidding all over the place like a bumper car.

A wolf-whistle sounded, drawing me out of the little bubble I'd sunken into.

Slowly, I pulled away from Logan to see who was passing by. Nash and Max strolled along the sidewalk up ahead, and Nash gave me an up-nod. I slung an arm around Logan, not hesitating to make it clear where he and I stood.

"I don't think I'll ever get used to that," he said, fanning himself.

"Hmm?" I asked as I guided us in the direction of Jake's. Better we get our food and get the hell out before the rest of the town ruined our date.

"The way you claim me wherever we are," he murmured. "I would have never suspected Cooper Ellis to be a PDA guy."

"What can I say?" I grabbed the door with my free hand, bringing it open. "You've always made me a little crazy."

Logan shook his head, a small grin on his lips that was softer than his usual ones. We stepped inside, and the music from Jake's filtered our way at once, along with the murmur of conversation from the folks already here. Early afternoon and the place wasn't packed yet, not like it would be tonight.

"Logan Nichols, you've got some explaining to do," a familiar voice sounded.

The temptation to turn the other way and walk out was high, but we weren't going to be able to get around this one.

Penny stood there staring at us, her jaw dropped.

I glanced to Logan. "Did you not tell your best friend?"

He scratched his nape. "Look, we never set terms or talked about who we were letting know. I'm still waiting for someone to jump out and tell me I'm getting pranked." The way his vulnerabilities slipped through now made me wonder how I'd missed this side of him for years.

"I told Gramps," I said, arching a brow.

He opened his mouth and shut it. "Well, damn."

Penny stopped in front of us. "Hey, Coop. Don't mind if I take a moment with my supposed best friend."

"I'll get the takeout," I said, letting go of Logan. Rye was working tonight, and the moment he saw me approach, he reached beneath the bar.

"Your order's right here," he said, pulling out two bags with Styrofoam containers. I handed my card over, and he rang me up quick. "Sure you don't want to take the back exit out before your boy gets mobbed?" He tilted his head in the direction of Logan, who accumulated people by the second. Penny was talking loudly enough that "can't believe" could be heard over the rest of the din, and I saw Gina and Mrs. Loyola approach, which meant Logan would be cornered for god knew how long.

No goddamn way. This was my evening with him, at long fucking last.

"I'll take you up on the suggestion," I said to Rye before grabbing the food.

Time to get the hell out. In a few quick strides, I was back over to Logan, and I looped my arm through his. "Hey, ladies. Let's have this conversation at a later date." With that, I whisked Logan in the opposite direction we came, heading toward the back exit of the bar, which wasn't as crowded as the entrance. Ben waved in our direction like he might approach, but I simply tipped my head his way before picking up speed.

"Are we on the run?" Logan asked, a laugh bubbling out of him. "What the hell has you charging out of here like your ass is on fire?"

We burst through the back doors of Jake's Tap, but I didn't let go of Logan's arm, continuing to lead us. Once we got to my car and away from this nosy goddamn town, we could relax.

"Because this is our date, and if we don't leave soon, it's going to be disrupted by half the town," I muttered.

Logan ran his tongue over his lower lip, which only highlighted it more. "All the possessiveness is so damn hot, babe."

"Just get in my truck," I said, loping toward it. I caught sight of a familiar beat-up Ford pulling in front of Jake's Tap and knew we had to floor it. If Jordan caught us here, he would be relentless, and we'd never escape.

"So romantic," Logan said as he looped around to the passenger's side. The slam of the doors echoed, and I settled in the driver's seat, leaning back to drop our food there.

Once I got the keys in the ignition and the engine rumbled, something inside me calmed. Honestly, I'd never had this pulsing need to get a guy or girl alone like this in the past, but the more we kept getting interrupted, the crazier I was going. My truck cut across the asphalt with ease, placing the main stretch of town in my rearview.

"Where are we heading?" Logan asked, leaning back in the seat. "Is this another of your obscure nature spots to bury me in the woods?"

I cast him a sidelong glance. "Yes, I'm going to ask you on a date to murder you somewhere outdoorsy. Does nature terrify you or something?"

"Look, not all of us are Mr. Hikes For Breakfast with his steel-toed boots and Wranglers," Logan said, lifting his hands in the air.

I snorted. "Let me guess—you're more quiet place to read or drinks in town?"

"Well, now you're just stereotyping." Logan's voice was as wry and sarcastic as ever, but unlike in the past when his comments used to irritate me, I'd started cataloging all those little details. The man fascinated me, and the more I learned about him, the more I wanted to find out.

I let out a long, slow breath as the reality that we were alone at last settled over me. "We're going to this peaceful spot at Starlight Ranch. I do some work for them, and they gave me permission to swing by."

"Mmm, so you're saying you've got connections," Logan said, waggling his brows.

Fuck, the amount I grinned was ridiculous. "Nothing to shout home about," I said, tapping the steering wheel. "Though, I've got some news about Gramps and Ms. Hendricks."

"Oh, do tell," Logan said, vaulting forward in his seat.

"Caught the two of them making out in the stacks," I said with a smirk. "Also might've mentioned to Gramps that we were seeing each other on my way out."

"The town's going to be disappointed you're not even trying to deny it," Logan said, his tone a bit lighter. "Where's the drama there?"

My brows drew together. "Are you okay with us telling people?" I'd assumed he'd want the reassurance since at every turn he was making comments like I might vanish. Given his history, I could understand why. Quiet settled from his side of the car, and my gut knotted. Had I misread the situation?

"You have no idea how long I've wanted this," Logan said, his voice barely above a whisper. "But if this is going to be a fling or a few dates only to call it quits..."

I was tempted to pull over to the side of the road, just to be able to look him in the eyes. "You've known me a long while, Logan Nichols—long enough to understand when I'm serious about something, I'm all in. There's no fling or few dates here. I want you as my boyfriend." My heart thumped hard as I waited for him to respond, going crazy with not being able to scrutinize his reaction.

"Damn you, Coop," he murmured. I yanked my focus from the road for a second to glance his way. A glimpse was all I needed. His eyes were shiny, and his lopsided grin was the sort of vulnerable I'd fast become addicted to. "You have no idea how long I've imagined hearing those words."

"Since high school, I'm guessing," I teased. The sign for Starlight Ranch rose into view, and I pulled onto the unpaved dirt drive. Clouds of dust kicked out around me as I headed to the overlook. It was by a small pond, and the view of the Grand Tetons stole my breath every time.

"Though you're apparently dense enough it took ten years for you to realize I was flirting," Logan responded, his usual snark returning.

I drove off-road over to the spot, the truck bouncing as we got closer to our destination. The need to just kiss the fuck out of this man rose higher and higher, and I wanted to capture those brief flickers of Logan being real with me before he tucked them away. When I put the car in park, I didn't wait. I wrapped my hand around Logan's nape, crushing our lips together.

I drank in the taste of him, sweetness and heat. After I'd spent years trying to click with all the wrong people and never being enough, either being too boring, too particular, I'd finally met the man who was my match. Because Logan had seen me at my worst for a damn long time—and he fucking liked me anyway. Logan let out a low moan that vibrated against my mouth, and the sound traveled straight to my cock.

I pulled back, running my finger under his chin so our eyes met. "Yes, I'm fucking dense. Because if I'd been paying better attention, I would've realized just how perfect you were years ago."

Logan's throat bobbed, and his breath hitched. "Bullshit," he said, his voice coming out hoarse. "I'm a bunch of problems wrapped up in a trench coat."

"Well, maybe I want to make you my problem," I responded, a grin rising to my lips.

"Fuck, that was cheesy as shit, Coop." Still, his grin was fucking radiant. I ran my thumb across his lower lip, loving the way he shivered in response.

"Okay, we need to get out of here, or I'm about to burn up any goodwill I have and fuck you in this car," I muttered, drawing away. I grabbed the takeout from the back, the keys from the ignition, and hopped out of my car.

The winds were bracing out here, the sort that stung but also the kind that reminded me I was alive. I walked over to Logan and threaded our hands together, leading him in the direction of the pond. The water rippled slightly from the strength of the breezes, but it reflected the broad blue sky overhead dotted with puffball clouds. The Grand Tetons cut across the horizon, their majestic peaks as breath stealing as they'd always been. However, the sight of Logan walking by my side, a smile continuing to twitch at his lips, beat out even the grandeur around us.

My heart squeezed tight at the sight, and the urgency that had been riding me all week settled at last.

"It's beautiful out here," Logan said as we came to a stop right by the big rocks dotting the pond. He cast me a wry look. "I know the real reason you whisked me away to somewhere remote."

"Oh? Why's that?" I asked, settling on the surface of one of the rocks and drawing Logan beside me.

"Only way to get a little peace," Logan said, those dark eyes piercing right through me. Because he *saw* me. "You're in high demand in town—oldest brother of the Ellis clan, handyman to half of Collier's Creek, leatherworker. Everyone wants something from you." I shook my head, in a little disbelief at how well Logan knew me. Before I could say anything, he continued. "Maybe that's why I'm in town so often—kid from the outskirts, I just wanted to feel like a part of it all."

I squeezed his hand, which was still interlaced with mine. "You are. You might not see it, but you've made your mark across this place, Lo. God only knows, you've made your mark on me."

"From sheer irritation?" he said, his eyes gleaming, even though he couldn't hide the bit of raw and real he'd given me, pieces of himself I was learning to cherish.

"That for sure," I said, settling back and letting the crisp air clear my mind. "But you don't ever need to worry about your place in town—because you're mine."

Logan lapsed into quiet, but when I glanced over, the soft warmth in his dark eyes had me holding my tongue. Instead, I simply squeezed his hand again, and he squeezed back. The pond reflected the late-afternoon beams of the sun, hazy and golden, same as the warm feelings rising through my veins. The white caps of the Grand Tetons were so bright I almost needed to look away, and the crisp breeze carried the scent of fall, of promises.

Our food was probably getting cold, but after all the bickering we'd done for years, Logan and I had finally found the right words.

Chapter Eighteen

Logan

The date out at Starlight Ranch had been perfect—almost too perfect. We'd eaten our burgers and then lazily made out by the pond until it was too cold to stay there. I wouldn't risk my nuts to try to fuck out in the wilderness, and besides, I'd earned a bed at this point.

Coop drove into the driveway of his rancher, a cozy house I'd only ever been to a handful of times for Ellis family events I'd been invited to. The one thing that had me nervous the guillotine would fall was the fact that earlier today I'd received the email I'd been waiting for.

I'd gotten the remote job.

Which would mean an end of working with Gramps but also moving out of Aunt Beth's. However, it might also spell the end of being included in the Ellis family as well. Despite how hot the connection had been flaring between Coop and I, the loyalty he had for his family was unparalleled. I still wasn't sure if taking this job would wreck us before we'd even begun.

"What's got you so deep in thought?" Coop asked as he tugged open the passenger's door. "We've been parked for a minute here."

"Climate change," I deadpanned, and he shot me one of those grumpy looks I'd grown so fond of over the years. Seemed like I was still plenty capable of annoying him.

"Well, if you're done pondering climate change, I've got something special for you inside," he said, his gaze turning molten. My adrenaline surged at the sight, and my cock took interest. Cooper Ellis was just one surprise after another, and I still couldn't believe most of them. My years of daydreams had included some hot-as-hell fantasies, but I'd never expected the kinky streak or how physically affectionate he was.

"Is the surprise your cock?" I asked, hopping out of the car and following him to the front door. "Because I hate to break it to you, but I've already seen it a few times." The cobbled path to the front house was meticulous, and I didn't doubt Coop had done the handiwork himself. The front door was a pretty rustic red, and the white siding with the gray tiled roof created a charming, picturesque effect, even at nighttime when illuminated by the front light.

"Well, surprise ruined then," Coop said, holding the door open for me and gesturing inside. "Guess you're in for a disappointing night."

I shot him a look as I sauntered past, making sure to put some extra swing into my hips. "Oh, honey, with me involved, there's no way it can be disappointing."

Coop's snort echoed from behind me, and he flicked the lights on. His main sitting area was just as cozy as the outside, with black couches against the cream walls, a TV, and another room with a large dining room table I was pretty sure he'd built by hand too. Fuck, this man was everything I'd dreamed about—stability, the perfect flavor of dominant, and good with his hands in every sense of the phrase. I'd be lying to myself if I said I hadn't already fallen for him. Truth was, I'd been half in love with him since high school.

And once he met me midway? My heart hadn't stood a chance.

"The bedroom's down the hall," he said. "First door to the right."

"Mighty presumptuous we are," I called back, even though I didn't hesitate in my stride. Hell yes I wanted to get fucked so hard my toes went numb, and I knew this man could deliver. And this time, we'd be able to collapse into a heap afterward, not needing to cover a jizz spot on the fly or hurry to get clothed because his best friend busted in.

His best friend better not bust in tonight.

"Kai's not going to swing over, is he?" I asked as I reached the doorway, glancing back.

Coop let out a snort. "Not if he values his life. Though, just in case, I say we lock the bedroom door. Too many people have the key to my house."

My heart gave a little twist at the idea I might someday be included in that mix. I wanted to hold back—no one had stuck around in my life for long, and I'd been a bit too much for the ones who had—and yet I hurtled forward regardless. I couldn't put the brakes on this relationship if I wanted to.

Coop shut the door behind him, and the little click of the lock echoed through the room, sending a shiver down my spine. My cock was growing harder by the second, and my mind reeled with the idea that he had more in store for us. The adventurous side of him had been unexpected, mostly because he seemed to be the down-to-earth, rational one amongst his family. But I sure as hell wasn't complaining.

"Strip down and get on the bed," Coop commanded, his voice the sensual husky tone that immediately got my heart rate up.

"And what if I don't want to?" I asked, wanting to push a little. As much as everything inside me melted the moment Coop started looking my way with heat in his eyes, snark was part of my DNA.

"Then I'll make you," Coop said, striding toward me nice and slow. The slight bit of growl in his voice got my adrenaline pumping, and

I had to resist just stripping and following orders—mostly because I wanted to see what he'd do. Everything about this man thrilled me to the point of no return.

I backed away a few steps, a smile curving my lips as our eyes caught. Pure fire. My heart thudded so hard I could hear it in my ears, and I came to a sudden stop as the backs of my knees hit the bed.

"Should've figured you'd be a brat," he murmured, continuing his approach until there was mere inches between us. The air was blisteringly hot, and I sucked in a desperate lungful. Coop grabbed my chin, jerking my focus onto him, and a bolt of lust coursed through my system. His rough touch, the way his blue eyes blazed, all of it had me going out of my mind with need.

"Well, where's the fun in obeying?" I managed, my hands balled into fists at my sides to keep myself from reaching out to touch him. Fuck, I wanted to run my hands over the ridges of muscle along his skin, the sexy dips and valleys of his torso. My mouth watered for the weight of his cock again, but honestly, I would take any damn thing he wanted to give me.

He placed his palm on the center of my chest and gave a firm push. Before I could stop myself, I went careening backward to land onto the mattress. Coop was on top of me a moment later, pressing his lips against mine.

I let out a low moan and writhed beneath him in a playful attempt to struggle as he pinned my wrists overhead with one damn hand, ravaging my mouth in the process. We ground our fronts together, the friction so-damn-good even though I needed more, more, more. We'd finally found time alone, undisturbed, and I wanted to savor this, to memorize the feel of his body against mine. And yet every time I was around him, my skin buzzed, the desire for him palpable in the air.

He reached between us, found the button of my jeans, and flicked it open. Next went the zipper and then he tugged my boots off, then my jeans. The fabric was so tight around my legs that he let go of my wrists and stood on his knees to try to drag it down. Served me right for trying to wear the jeans that made my ass look good.

"Take them off and lie on the bed. You disobey, and you don't get to come," he said before rising and slipping off the bed with a creak. My curiosity was piqued, and I peeled off my jeans and briefs and then started unbuttoning my shirt. Coop stalked over to his tall dresser and plucked something from the surface. When he turned back in my direction, I caught sight of the leather strips in his hand. If my cock wasn't already hard enough, the sight would've done me in.

Something about a man with leather...goddamn.

I tossed my shirt to the pile before scooting up on the bed, all too aware of the way Coop stared at me. His eyes were ablaze, the pupils dilated, and the slight hitch of his breath as he scanned me over obliterated any defenses.

Part of me wanted to roll off the bed, to push back just to see what he'd do, but the stronger part of me needed to come with him tonight. To feel our bodies crush together, to soak in that bliss and lose myself in him.

"How do you feel about being bound up?" he asked. I tugged at my balls to keep from coming on the spot.

"Yes, please," I murmured, spreading my legs wide. His hungry gaze roved there, and when he licked his lips, all I could remember was the sinful way his mouth had felt against me when he'd devoured my ass.

"Good," he said, bringing one set of the simple leather restraints up to my wrists, which were lying overhead. Coop stripped in quick, economical motions, until his clothes were on the floor and his gorgeous body was on complete display.

He straddled me, his thick cock resting right on my chest as he worked in deft motions to bind my wrists in the soft leather. With his thighs straddling me on either side, I was about to expire from how fucking turned on I was. His body bracketing mine was hot as hell, and the leather cuffs he wrapped around my wrists fit perfectly.

The idea of being completely at his mercy ticked every single one of my boxes.

Coop reached down and grabbed my right ankle, wrapping another restraint around it, and a moment later, he looped it through an extender piece at the cuff on my right wrist, binding them together. Holy hell. Pre-cum dripped down my cock, my balls aching. He was going to tie my wrists and ankles together, leaving me spread open for him. My lashes fluttered, and my breaths came in a little faster with the sheer rush of lust pumping hot through my veins right now.

He made quick work of binding my other ankle and wrist together, which left my legs spread, my hole exposed. The vulnerability of the position had me floating, my cock so achingly hard I could scream. I gave a light tug to the restraints, loving the rebound back, the supple leather with the strong scent amping up my arousal.

"Did you do a rush order on these?" I asked, marveling at how comfortable they were, how the fit seemed perfect.

"Made them last night," he said, his voice the slightest bit gruff. His cheeks flushed a little bit, giving off the telltale hint Coop was embarrassed. "Haven't gotten that into a project in a while, so I kept going with it."

I licked my lips, trying to ignore this heady adrenaline making my mind whirl from the sheer force of this attraction between us. Except it was more than that—these past few weeks it had deepened in a way I'd always dreamed of but never thought would be a reality. Everything had moved at a whiplash speed, to the point I still had to double-check this was happening, that I hadn't just imagined it all.

Yet, Coop was like that—black and white, and he didn't waste time in those rare instances he did change his mind.

"I love these," I murmured with another tug to the restraints as I offered a little more of myself. I'd been holding those pieces hostage for years, as if waiting for the right person to come along. It was like a part of me had recognized Coop was that person all along—it had just taken him seeing *me* to realize.

"Fuck, you look so damn pretty bound up for me," he said, brushing the tips of his fingers along my hole. A full-body shudder wracked through me, my cock so hard it was leaking. The deep tone of his voice, the intensity in his eyes—all of it launched me higher into the stratosphere. My body hummed, my skin so sensitive due to being spread open like this, helpless to this man. "Color?" he asked.

I shot him a look. "How many ways do I need to say green?" Still, I appreciated his check-in. Bondage usually got me floaty faster than most kinks, and even something simple like this, having my wrists bound to my ankles, made my body hum, my brain quieting faster than normal.

"You're such a brat," he murmured before cupping my ass and lifting it up. A moment later, the hot, wet sensation of his tongue dragged up across my hole, and my back arched. Coop didn't give pause—no, he just set to devouring my ass with the patient determination he showed everything. His hands gripped me tight, and the overwhelming pleasure that radiated through me had my cock achingly hard. But I couldn't do a damn thing about it. My hands curled into fists, nails biting into my palms as Coop ravaged me, spit dripping down my crack.

My breaths came out in quickened pants, and the waves of bliss radiating through me were so intense I didn't want him to stop, even as the need to come coiled tight.

Coop reached between my spread legs and wrapped his hand around my cock. A shout escaped from me, loud enough to reverberate through the room. Unlike all the other times, now I didn't have to try to muffle them.

"Fuck, yes, yes, yes," I panted as he continued to nip and suck at my hole while he stroked my cock. His tongue burrowed in, and I put the new restraints to the test as I bucked my hips, writhing but unable to move much. My lashes fluttered as my eyes kept rolling back from how damn good his mouth felt—fuck, this man was pure magic. Adrenaline coursed right through me, and my balls began to draw up.

"I'm going to come," I choked out, and Coop let go of my cock. I swallowed hard as the tension receded the slightest bit, but with the way he ate me out, I was still writhing from pleasure. Sweat prickled across my forehead, and I panted like a bitch in heat as he continued to devour me, like he was made for this. He wrapped his hand around my length again, giving me another stroke that sent me shuddering.

My whole body reacted again, but like before, there was nowhere to go. My mind reeled at being at his mercy like this, and the sight of his head bobbing between my legs, the way his big hand teased pre-cum up and down my cock, how the scent of leather surrounded me all got me so hot I couldn't take it anymore.

"Coop," I cried out, tilting my head back. His tongue was relentless, spearing me open until I thought I might just explode into his hand.

The bastard let go again.

I whined. "Fucking hell, you monster."

He nipped the inside of my thigh. "That's the fun of this."

"Wouldn't it be more fun if you were sticking your thick cock inside me?" I asked, batting my lashes. Before I could try to entice him further, he set to destroying me with his tongue and hands. Pleasure rolled through me in waves as he drove his tongue inside me all while he began to jerk me off anew. Each stroke had me closer to coming, and my slit was oozing pre-cum like it was a job at this point.

"I just need to come," I gritted out, the intensity climbing to the point I was going to scream. And yet all I could do was lie here given the way he'd bound me up. I huffed out a breath before another long moan ripped from my throat as he brought me so close to the edge.

"You know the rules, baby," he murmured. "You come on my cock."

Fuck, heat raced through my whole body. Coop let go again, and I wanted to sob. Except then he pushed up from the mattress and nabbed a condom and lube from his dresser. Coop positioned himself in front of me on his knees as he rolled the condom on the sizeable length he was about to thrust deep inside me. My mouth fucking watered at the sight, just a reflex at this point.

"How badly do you want this?" he asked, lubing up his cock before bringing the tip to my hole.

I licked my lips, tempted to mouth off. When his gaze met mine though, all the teasing faded away. The seriousness in those eyes ensnared me, and suddenly we were talking about something else altogether. My heart thumped hard, and the ache bloomed in my chest. Tonight, I couldn't deny him.

"I need you."

Three simple words that came out as a whisper, but I didn't hold anything back.

"God, you're so gorgeous," he murmured. He pushed inside me, the glide nice and smooth with the amount he'd rimmed me into oblivion. My eyes rolled back again as he thrust inside me completely, that fullness something I'd been craving from the moment he bent me over his desk and fucked me until I couldn't see straight. Unlike that time though, tonight, I was fully exposed—lying on my back, face-to-face, and my heart bared to him.

It should terrify me—and it did—yet I'd also never felt safer.

"Spread out for me like a pretty slut," he murmured, running his palms along my thighs. "You look so fucking hot."

A shiver raced through my spine, and Coop grabbed me by the thighs as he began to move. All thought obliterated from my brain when he slammed back in. Stars burst through me, my vision blanking out as he landed on my prostate. Strands of his dark hair plastered against his sweaty forehead, and his mouth was slightly open as he concentrated on fucking me into oblivion. When Coop picked up the pace, he didn't mess around with slow or sweet.

No, the man drove into me with a brutal fucking I'd feel for days.

I loved it.

My world was reduced to the squeeze of the bands around my wrists and my ankles. The scent of sweat and leather ripe in the air. The shattered grunts and moans that erupted from both of us. The smack of skin against skin with every deep thrust inside.

And so, so much blinding pleasure.

My cock was leaking, my balls aching, desperate for release, but I couldn't touch them if I tried. I was completely at Coop's mercy, and he wouldn't let me come until he was ready. Wetness pooled at my eyes from the sheer intensity of the bliss hitting me, how fucking out of my mind he got me. This man knew how to strip me down and build me anew in one sweep, and I was so addicted I never wanted this to end.

My balls kept tensing up, but I just needed his hand on my cock to get me spilling over. I sucked in lungful after lungful of the tense air, the heat burning within us exploding outward. Coop's gaze remained fixed on me, a softness there that directly contrasted to the ferocious way he fucked. My heart thudded so hard it was louder than anything else.

This man was my end game. He always had been.

"Come for me, Lo," he commanded, and he gripped my length, giving purposeful strokes.

Those words and his touch were all I needed.

My balls drew up, and at-fucking-last, the orgasm barreled through me. Cum exploded from me, spurting all over the place as the coiled tension released in one glorious sweep. The intensity stole me away, my fingers and toes numbing from the force and my breath snagged in my throat.

A second later, Coop thrust deep, and a low, long moan escaped him. He remained buried there as his cock throbbed inside me, his own orgasm catching up to him. I let my eyes drift shut, and the lazy waves of pleasure ambled through me. Our breaths burst through the air, harsh and heavy in the quiet that followed after all the frenzy, all the movement.

The soft rustle of leather signaled first that Coop was releasing me from the bonds, and the straps fell away—first from my right side, then my left. My legs dropped to the bed, my arms too as I sank boneless into the mattress, not giving a damn that my chest was splattered with cum.

Slowly, Coop pulled out of me, and the creak of the mattress sounded as he rose to tie off the condom and get rid of it. I tracked him stepping out of the bedroom, but I couldn't make myself move. The orgasm had knocked out any remaining ability to be upright. Coop returned a moment later with a wet washcloth, and before I could reach for it, he was already wiping down my chest, around my hole, gentle, careful strokes that made my chest flutter.

"Make some room," Coop said as he settled onto the bed beside me, nudging me over from the full-out sprawl I'd been doing in the middle of the mattress. Relief settled in my chest that he wasn't kicking me out—though, it would've been out of character for the man, given his determination to get me alone in the first place.

I curled to the side, and his arm slung around my waist as he brought himself flush behind me. He nuzzled into the side of my neck, consuming my senses. My heart grew so full it might break as the comfort of this moment filled a part of me I hadn't realized was still hollow.

All I knew was that I couldn't lose this man.

The potential here, the safe place he offered to land, the way he made my heart soar—this wasn't just everything I'd secretly wanted.

Coop was the connection I'd spent a lifetime searching for.

Chapter Nineteen

Cooper

I'd expected to wake up with Logan still in bed, but when I cracked my eyes open, the sheets were empty beside me. Disappointment settled in my chest until I caught the unmistakable scent of bacon wafting in from the open door to my room.

Maybe he hadn't left.

I pushed out of bed and pulled on my boxer briefs, not bothering with anything else before I sauntered in to investigate. Logan stood in my kitchen, in nothing but his briefs, which cupped the delicious ass I couldn't seem to get enough of. To be real though, I just couldn't get enough of him. His snark that turned sweet when we fucked, his sharp mind that always seemed to be two steps ahead, and how he brought out an adventurous side of me I actually liked.

Turned out the perfect man for me had been right under my nose the entire time.

He glanced up from the skillet of eggs and bacon he tended to, a few strands of his blond hair drifting over his forehead.

"Should've figured you were already up," I murmured, walking up to him. Seeing him here in my space felt right, maybe part of the frantic push all week to get him in it. Because this sight clicked a puzzle piece in my brain. I placed my hands around his hips and kissed into the crook of his neck before licking to take a taste of his salty skin.

"Guess you just want your bacon to burn," Logan said, the attempt at teasing falling flat due to the note of tension in his voice.

I pulled back, my brows drawing together. "Did something happen?"

His shoulders tightened.

My mind whirled to last night. Should I have checked in more with the restraints we used? Had I done a shit job at aftercare? My hands fell from his waist, and I stepped away, needing to know what was going on.

"Fuck," Logan said, turning the burner off and placing the spatula down. He scrubbed at his face before he whipped toward me. "You're going to break up with me."

I crossed my arms, wariness prickling up my spine. "Why don't you let me decide that?"

"I might have to leave the bookstore," he blurted out, pacing in a different direction—away from me. "I mean, I got the job, but I haven't taken it yet. I don't want to leave. I love working there, but I can't keep living with Aunt Beth, and I've got way too much baggage—"

I stepped up to him and placed a finger over his lips. "Wait." My brain tried to break down the babble in chunks, but none of that spelled the need to break up. Gramps would be sad to lose Logan as an employee, but what did that have to do with us?

Logan's eyes were wide, panicked, and he buzzed. My heart twisted tight.

"You don't think I'd break up with you over needing to take a different job, do you?" I asked slowly.

Logan's bob of his neck with his swallow answered the question. "I know how loyal you are to your family..."

I cupped his cheeks, bringing his face up so our eyes met. "You realize since we're dating, that loyalty extends to you too, right? Before we continue this conversation, I'm going to make this crystal clear—I'm not going to keep you from pursuing your goals. That's not what a good boyfriend does. I'm here with you either way."

Logan's eyes grew glassy, and I couldn't help but dip in to brush my lips against his. My chest tightened. This man. He'd been through so much I'd never realized about.

I pulled away, needing to parse through the rest of this. "So, is this job something you're really interested in? And what do you mean by too much baggage?"

Logan scrubbed at his face with his palms again. "Ugh, so when Mom passed, she also left a lot of medical debt. I'm chipping away at it bit by bit, but that's the reason I'm still living with my aunt, who's not super fond of me. The editing work I do isn't steady enough to bolster my income at the shop. Gramps pays me fair wages, but if I want to survive, I need to make more."

Fuck. I ran my thumb along the side of his face. "You've been shouldering so much by yourself for so long, haven't you."

The urge to dive in and fix his problems reared in a big way, and unlike the trivial bullshit my siblings brought to my door, these were hard life calls. We'd just started dating, so it was a bit early to tell him to move in with me, even though my heart was racing forward in that direction. However, Logan had single-handedly set me on the right path with my own business woes.

I wanted to do something for him.

"That's a cute way of saying I'm a certifiable disaster," Logan said, infusing his tone with snark, even though his edges were softer than normal.

"You already spent ten years trying to keep me at a distance," I said, letting my hand drift down to his hip. "Those tactics don't work anymore."

"Damn," he muttered, even though he leaned in against my chest as I gripped his hip, drawing him close. "I haven't taken the job yet, but they want an answer by Tuesday. I don't want it, but I don't see another way."

My heart thumped a little harder, my mind reeling.

He might not, but I did.

Because with how self-reliant Logan was, I could piece together there was one avenue he hadn't tried. One I wouldn't hesitate to pursue.

"Can you do me a favor?" I asked. "Don't give them a response until Tuesday."

Logan's eyes narrowed. "The company's in New York, so good luck setting it on fire."

I snorted. "I don't want to bring up anything in case this idea doesn't pan out, so let's just table the discussion and enjoy our morning."

"Now with a hundred percent less looming heartbreak," Logan muttered.

I shook my head as I gave his hip a squeeze. "I don't care how many times I have to reassure you—I'm serious—"

"Story of your life," Logan jumped in.

"—about us," I continued, leveling him with a look. "And I'm not going anywhere, Logan."

He leaned in and pressed a sweet kiss to my cheek, the sort that made my chest ache. "Thank you," he murmured before he stepped away over to the skillet. "Now let's eat this breakfast before it goes cold."

"I'm not complaining," I said, heading over to my cupboards to grab plates, "but how the hell are you up so early after what we did last night?"

"Stamina." Logan winked. "Haven't you heard of it?"

"Fucking brat," I growled, even as my heart bounced. When our eyes met, his twinkled, and my lips twitched, unable to keep a scowl on my face. I set the plates on my kitchen table with a clink and reached around to squeeze Logan's ass while he carried over the skillet of eggs. His lashes fluttered, and my cock already started to thicken at the feel of the meaty handful.

Logan shoveled out the eggs, then snagged the bacon too, dishing that out. Toast popped up from the toaster with a ping, and within seconds, a full breakfast was ready. My stomach rumbled at the sight of it. I lifted my fork, prepared to dig the fuck in, but my gaze halted on the sight of Logan sitting across from me, leaning back in his seat.

His hair was mussed from sleep, and he was only in his briefs, a few reddened marks and bruises on display across his skin from last night. The sight alone was hot as hell, but his presence in my kitchen, in my life was the gamechanger here.

I'd always been a simple man—wanting to pursue my craft, take care of my family, and enjoy life in this crazy little town crammed with so many unique personalities. However, there'd always been a sense of completion I'd been searching for, something missing.

And he was sitting right across the table from me.

Chapter Twenty

Logan

I'd been on edge all day today.

The last thing Coop had said about the job situation was "trust me," and I did, but at the same point, the day of reckoning was tomorrow. My shift at the bookstore had been agonizing, too slow to be a distraction, and every back-and-forth thought I had about the decision remained inconclusive. The only relief I clutched onto now was that no matter the choice, it wouldn't change me and Coop.

After our date night, I'd stayed over there last night as well, and Coop seemed in no hurry to excise me. Which was dangerous, because if we kept up this rate, I would just move my belongings in one by one until I lived there permanently. Fuck, splitting rent would be a thousand times cheaper than going it alone—and might even allow me to stay at the bookstore. But as much as I fantasized about it, I wasn't going to impose on Coop this early into our relationship.

And I needed a surefire solution.

I settled into the desk and cracked open my laptop. An email had come in on the tab I kept open 24/7. Before I could click it though, the bell to the front door jangled.

My attention snapped up as I shut the lid of my laptop. In strode Gramps and Coop, and my stomach twisted. Had Coop told him about the situation I was in? I dreaded having the conversation with Gramps, but it had to come from me. Was this where Gramps took the decision out of my hands and fired me?

The idea made bile rise in my throat, and the jitters started to travel up through me. Maybe that was the answer right there.

"What are you two doing here?" I asked, aware my voice rose three octaves too high.

Coop had his signature glower on, and even Gramps didn't have the normal twinkle in his eye. I remained planted, not wanting to show that my knees were all but knocking at this point.

"Coop filled me in," Gramps said, his gaze softening as he came to a halt in front of the desk. "I didn't know about all the bills you were shouldering, Logan."

I chewed on my lower lip, not trusting myself to say anything. Part of me was a little pissed at Coop for spilling my secrets, but he was doing it because I refused to ask for help—from anyone but him apparently. We were too alike in that regard.

"If you want to stay, I'm happy to have you," he continued. "But I also understand if you need to leave too."

Hearing those words aloud settled something inside me. Gramps looked at me with the acceptance I'd longed for, that just because I might not be able to continue working here didn't mean I'd be losing the friendship we'd cultivated.

"However," Coop stepped in. "Gramps here isn't telling you everything. If you do want to stay, you have a way to do that. Check your email."

The adrenaline was pumping through my whole body now as I cracked my laptop back open. The tab that had been waiting for me before they'd arrived was in view, and I zeroed in on the email.

Freelance Editing Opportunity

My heart thumped so hard it drowned out most other sounds as I looked up to Coop. "What did you do?"

He crossed his arms in his signature move as he met my gaze. "What you wouldn't. I asked Gramps for help."

I still hadn't clicked on the email, the hope almost unbearable at this point. "What sort of help?"

"We work with a lot of small presses," Gramps said. "I know you'd never take advantage of those connections for your own gain, which says a lot about you, son. However, I have no problem doing it on your behalf. Those publishers like working with you here, and a few of them had openings for editors. Astra Press was the first one to reach out, but I suspect you'll be getting more emails to follow. *If* this is what you want."

I clicked on the email, skimming through it. Everything Gramps said was true—Astra had asked me to send a few samples over, and if they liked what they saw, they'd be sending steady work my way. My pulse roared.

I could stay.

My smile broke out unbidden, and I couldn't hide the sheer joy bubbling up inside me. "There's nowhere else I'd rather be than here, at Ellis Books."

Coop's eyes crinkled, the warmth there flushing through me. This fucking man. I loved him with everything in me, and I needed him to know that, right this second.

"Good," Gramps said, clapping a hand on my shoulder as his boot let out a heavy thump. "Now get out of my seat—I'm going to take over the last hour here. You and my grandson have a date to get to."

"You say you want me to stay, yet you're kicking me out?" I teased, mostly to mask the liquid threatening to drop from my eyes. Fucking allergies.

"Don't mind him," Coop said. "He just wants to sneak Ms. Hendricks here again."

Gramps arched his bushy brow. "Don't be jealous because you've got a new boyfriend and things are already stale."

"So stale," I said, amusement welling in my chest. "Saltines level of boring."

Coop cuffed the back of my neck in a move that mixed possession and warning, making me swoon. Mmm, his dominant side was so damn fun. I couldn't wait to test him in every which way.

I hopped from the spot and left the chair open for Gramps, who took his time settling in. When he glanced up at me, the knowing in his eyes struck me dumb. He'd been rooting for me all along—well aware I had a raging crush on his grandson. And his support meant the world.

"I'd say welcome to the family—" Gramps leaned back in his seat "—but you were already a part of it."

My throat squeezed tight. These two men were determined to make me bawl my eyes out. "Okay, okay, let's get going," Coop said. "If we don't get to Jake's early, the regular dinner rush will come in, and there will be no peace."

"So we'll be eating like retirees instead," I shot back, sheer adrenaline thump, thump thumping through me.

Coop cast me another warning look, which I devoured.

"Saltines," Gramps said in a stage whisper, amusement crinkling his features.

Coop rolled his eyes and placed his hand on my low back, guiding me toward the door.

"Thanks, Gramps," I called, even though the words couldn't possibly contain the gratitude spilling out from me at this moment. Once we stepped outside the door of Ellis Books, Coop's lips were on mine.

I basked in his kiss, in the hungry way he consumed me right in the middle of the sidewalk in town. Sunlight beamed down on us, but none of those golden rays held a candle to the sheer joy bursting through me. Coop's hand pressed harder on my back, and he dipped his tongue in, drawing a low whimper from me.

When we broke for breath, his blue eyes glowed with warmth, with contentment, with everything I also felt.

"I love you, Cooper Ellis," I whispered, the words coming naturally despite the nerves they summoned. "I think I always have."

"Good," he murmured. "Because I'm keeping you. I love you too, Lo, and after ignoring the signs for so long, I don't want to waste another second."

I swallowed hard, memorizing everything about this moment. The crease between his brows that seemed to permanently be there, the serious turn of his lips, and the heat from his massive palm that imprinted on my back. This man had always been gorgeous enough to steal my breath away, but he was also loyal and kind and the sort of person to build a life with.

And he was all mine.

We ambled toward his car, since he had a hard-on for driving us places, and he hopped into the driver's seat while I made my way to the passenger's.

Coop started the ignition and turned to look at me. "You don't have some secret longing to go to Portland, do you?"

My brows drew together. "No, why?"

He grinned. "Good. Now let's hop over to Jake's before we get swarmed."

I settled back in the seat of his car as he drove down the street, one familiar place after another passing by through the car window. The hardware store, the coffee shop, the little B&B up the road—all footprints of this town that had worn a path in my heart. I'd always lived on the outskirts, never feeling like I fully fit in. However, through the years, I'd made my mark here, despite my unsteady footing.

And when the Ellis clan had opened their ranks to me, had welcomed me in through their doors, I'd found a family.

I glanced over to Coop, a hearthfire warmth settling in my chest that I knew would stay.

With Coop, I'd found my home.

Epilogue

Cooper

Six Months Later

I pulled up in front of Gramps's house, the big "Congratulations" banner out front.

Apparently he and Ms. Hendricks had been dating for a bit, and they'd just gotten engaged, something we were all thrilled about. Of course, the mention of engagements was making me a bit itchy to pull the trigger there. Life had been better than ever with Logan—enough that after three months, he'd moved in with me. Of course, we bickered plenty, same as always, but now when he poked and prodded, I had a fantastic solution to handling my brat—that ended with orgasms for both of us.

"I still say you should've let me take care of the banner." Logan sat in my passenger's seat, a constant fixture I hadn't realized how much I needed. My family's steady stream of ridiculous issues felt less weighty with someone else to share the burden with, and Logan's incessant cheerfulness, the way he loved to needle and tease me ended up lightening my days.

"You have a notoriously bad track record with banners," I said, shutting the engine off. The "honk if you love dick" banner had made a reappearance multiple times at my shop, but it didn't drive me as insane anymore. Especially not since Logan used it for marketing promo for the branch of my leatherworking trade that had taken off—kink toys and fetish wear. He'd been right on the mark, and my days of scraping for clients was in the past, all thanks to my brilliant, brilliant boyfriend.

He'd also taken off with his editing work, which allowed him to remain a fixture at Ellis Books. With Gramps getting remarried on the horizon, I knew he was looking to retire sooner rather than later, and I also knew what Logan didn't—that Gramps wanted him to take over the business.

"Okay, let's head in before they pull us out," I said, hopping out of my car. The slam of our doors echoed, and we walked up the stone path toward Gramps's house. The wall of sound hit us about halfway there, most of it coming from the backyard—shrieks, laughter, shouts. So many familiar sounds, all from my larger-than-average family.

"It's not too late to turn back around, is it?" I muttered, my introverted ass always cringing a little at the oncoming wave of chaos.

Logan rolled his eyes and slipped his hand in mine as we dipped past the side gate and stepped over to the April cookout we were having to celebrate. The sunny day had drawn everyone out from indoors, even though there was still a brisk breeze rolling through.

Gramps and Ms. Hendricks were sitting on the back porch along with my folks, and we caught their gazes and waved. Daisy's kids raced across the backyard shrieking, waving sticks at each other, and a few of the neighboring kids had joined in, creating one ragtag group of ruffians. Daisy and her husband Jared stood talking to Kyle from the hardware store and Arlo, a local who'd left years ago and recently moved back. Jordan had brought his roommates, and they all hung over by the beer while Henry was busy talking to the sheriff. Half of the town was coming to this shindig today, which made me want to run and hide even more.

I spotted Kai and Penny talking a few feet away, and they beckoned us over before we could get dragged in any other direction. I wasn't used to seeing Kai without Shelby at gatherings like these, but unfortunately the two had been rocky as of late. He'd even mentioned the idea of separating, which blew my mind with how long the two of them had been together.

"What took you guys so long?" Penny asked, and Logan and I just exchanged glances, a smirk rising to his lips. He'd been literally tied up while I fucked him until we were sweaty and spent—and then we'd gotten handsy in the shower.

"Nope, you don't want the answer to the question," Kai said, shaking his head. "I've seen and heard more than I can ever erase."

"Maybe if you knew boundaries," I started, and he lifted his middle finger.

"Hey," Sadie called out as she jogged up to us, out of breath and holding a cage with a blanket over it. I didn't bother hiding my groan. She'd lost Jordan Jr. a while ago—not dead, just fucking bolted, like a wild animal was guaranteed to do. Whatever she smuggled in that cage of hers couldn't be good news. She was still fixated on the idea of working with wild animals, and I planned on steering her in the direction of a parks and rec job instead of kidnapping them.

"Do I want to know?" I asked, and Logan tugged at my arm, an amused grin on his lips. Guaranteed, he already understood where my head was at.

"Meet Sadie Jr.," she said as she whipped off the blanket. A fisher sat inside, hissing. Great, more wild animals for the menagerie.

"You're acing this naming thing," Logan said, his eyes twinkling.

"Eh, it was on the fly," she said, her nose wrinkling as she looked at the large pile of shit in the corner of the cage.

"Take that beast to the corner of the yard right now," I said, pointing a finger to the spot opposite most of the crowds. "Away from the kids too." The last thing we needed was one of the munchkins to get mauled by a clearly disgruntled fisher.

"But I haven't showed him off to the rest of the family yet," she complained.

"How about you show Jordan?" Logan suggested, and I squeezed his hand in relief. They were a bit away from the rest of the crowds, and chances were, they'd find this amusing rather than a liability.

"Where's he at?" she asked, whipping around to find him. Before I could say anything else, she scampered off in that direction, like she was five and not in her mid-twenties.

I leaned in toward Logan and brushed a kiss to the side of his cheek. "I fucking love you."

His eyes met mine, those charming dark pools, and the depth of the affection there struck me on the spot, like it did every time. In a simple suggestion, he'd defused a family situation for me, same as the way he navigated social minefields with a grace I'd never managed. Some days, I couldn't believe how our situation had shifted, what we'd found together, but I knew enough to understand how lucky I was that this man belonged to me.

Logan Nichols was mine.

Pride welled in my chest along with love that had only grown stronger with each passing day. He was it for me—my forever—and I couldn't wait for the rest of our journey to unfold.

Afterword

Thank you for reading Logan and Coop's story, book four in Collier's Creek shared world! These six low angst, small town romances make for the perfect escape!

If you haven't read the other books in the series yet, start at the beginning of Collier's Creek! If you're looking for the next book, which features Arlo from the epilogue, it's Meeting Mr. Adorkable by Ali Ryecart.

Whether you prefer your books first person, high heat, and low angst with my Hot Under the Collar universe or medium angst, hurt/comfort, and third person with my Dungeons and Dating universe, there's plenty to dive into!

If you enjoyed the book, leave a review. Kind words are what us authors survive on, and I can tell you personally I treasure each and every one.

Collier's Creek Reading Order:
Best Kind of Awkward (Collier's Creek #1) by Becca Seymour
Mandatory Repairs (Collier's Creek #2) by Elle Keaton
Sheriff of the Creek (Collier's Creek #3) by Sue Brown
All the Wrong Pages (Collier's Creek #4) by Katherine McIntyre

Meeting Mr. Adorkable (Collier's Creek #5) by Ali Ryecart
Blue Skies (Collier's Creek #6) by Nic Starr

Also By

Want to find out where Coop's best friend Kai is going to end up, now that he's divorced?

Check out the kinky, queer found family that's about to welcome him in with open arms...
Pre-order Immersion Play, Leather and Lattes #1, today!

One bratty boy searching for somewhere to call home, one damaged Daddy Dom looking to escape his grief, and one kinky found family ready to help them both heal.

Micah's starting over. He left his old life in the middle of the night and showed up in San Francisco on a job tip from a friend. However, when Meg hires him at Whipped, he not only enters a new city but also a whole new world with this cozy crew of kinksters. And one man continues to catch his attention again and again.

Parker doesn't do relationships. After his mom died and his father became a shell of himself, he swore never to let anyone wreck him like that. Except Micah's gotten under his skin. The hot new barista at

Whipped isn't as vanilla as they all thought, and he's the brattiest boy that Parker could've ever dreamed of playing with. The connection between them? Incendiary.

However, the deeper their relationship grows, the more Micah's re-alizing he can't just be casual with Parker—not anymore. The man's made a mark on his soul, inspired dreams Micah had never even thought to reach for. But if Parker isn't willing to bend his rules to risk his heart, the two of them are definitely going to break.

Enter Whipped, a unique cafe that caters to coffee and kink addicts alike...

Also By

Want a low angst, high heat series featuring geeky found family, bears, and blue collar workers? Start the Hot Under the Collar series today with Sweat Connection!

One disaster bi single dad. One sexy plumber on a house call.

One hot-as-hell romance....

Rhys

If I was a hot mess before becoming a single dad, my life's pretty much an on-fire garbage can now.

Okay, maybe that's a tad melodramatic—my bestie/baby momma/ex-girlfriend is still awesome, currently in the throuple of her dreams. And my kiddo Sammy's amazing, albeit exhausting. I'm the one who's too intense and rambling, too obsessed with random trivia, too liable to set dinner on fire. Essentially, too much for any relationship.

However, when a hottie plumber drops by to fix our toilet—thanks, Sammy—and gives me his number? My luck might just be turning around.

Cole

After my dad moved to a retirement community, he left me with the big, old house I grew up in and a whole lot of loneliness.

I thought by now I'd be settled down, but no one's looking for the guy who likes long hikes with his dog, stargazing, and fixing shit around the house. They want fun, entertaining, flashy—not me.

Except when I give Rhys my private line for an emergency house call, I show up for the job to discover it's a date. It seems like I might've met the one man on earth who's just as interested as I am—if only we can find the guts to admit it.

Also By

Want hurt/comfort romances featuring a geeky, queer found family?
Read across the rainbow with the Dungeons and Dating series today!

Strength Check (Dungeons and Dating #1):
Roller derby, board games, and love collide in this roommates to lovers romance.

Wisdom Check (Dungeons and Dating #2):
Julian's boss is newly single, ridiculously hot, and looking his way. He's so screwed.

Intelligence Check (Dungeons and Dating #3):
Mason gives people too many chances, Hunter gives too few, but are they willing to take a chance on each other?

Constitution Check (Dungeons and Dating #4):
One night was all Kelly promised. One night was all Tabby offered. And yet one night wasn't nearly enough...

Dexterity Check (Dungeons and Dating #5):
Eli's sworn off irresponsible flirts, and Arjun's one of the worst—aggravating, provoking, and everything Eli can't resist.

Charisma Check (Dungeons and Dating #6):

Never fall for the straight guy—Jasper knows better. At least until his straight guy crush starts crushing back...

About the Author

Katherine McIntyre is a feisty chick with a big attitude despite her short stature. She writes stories featuring snarky women, ragtag crews, and men with bad attitudes—high chance for a passionate speech thrown into the mix. As a genderqueer geek who's always stepped to her own beat, she's made it her mission to write stories that represent the broad spectrum of people out there. Easily distracted by cats and sugar.